UNASHAMED

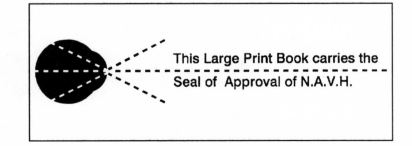

This Large Print Book carries the
Seal of Approval of N.A.V.H.

UNASHAMED

FRANCINE RIVERS

WALKER LARGE PRINT

An imprint of Thomson Gale, a part of The Thomson Corporation

THOMSON

GALE

Detroit • New York • San Francisco • New Haven, Conn. • Waterville, Maine • London • Munich

THOMSON
GALE

LIBRARY OF CONGRESS CATALOGING-IN-PUBLICATION DATA

Rivers, Francine, 1947–
    Unashamed / by Francine Rivers. — Large print ed.
      p. cm. — (A Lineage of grace series)
      ISBN 1-59415-141-5 (lg. print : alk. paper) 1. Rahab (Biblical figure) 2.
Large type books I. Title. II. Series: Rivers, Francine, 1947– Lineage of grace.
BS580.R3R58 2006
813'.54—dc22   2006008981

Published in 2006 in arrangement with Tyndale House Publishers, Inc.

Printed in the United States of America on permanent paper
10 9 8 7 6 5 4 3 2 1

To women who think a past of mistakes
ruins any chance of a joy-filled future.
Turn to Jesus and experience
the wonders He has waiting for you.

ACKNOWLEDGMENTS

No project is ever completed without the help of many people. I want to acknowledge my husband, Rick, who has supported and encouraged me from the beginning of my writing career.

I'd like to extend special thanks to Jane Jordan Browne and Scott Mendel for sharing their faith and resources. I'm also grateful to Liz Curtis Higgs and her husband, Bill, for sharing their extensive bibliography, and to Angela Elwell Hunt, my favorite superwoman. When I grow up, I want to be just like you.

I would also like to thank my editor, Kathy Olson, for her willingness to dive in and challenge me.

I extend special thanks to Jim and Charlotte Henderson for their gracious Washington State–style hospitality and to John and Merritt Atwood for the loan of their beautiful cottage on Whidbey Island for a brainstorming session with my dear friend, Peggy Lynch, who is writing the "Seek and Find" sections for these novellas. I would also like to thank Peggy for her willingness to be part of this project — and for making me dig deeper and deeper into Scripture to find the jewels waiting there.

INTRODUCTION

DEAR READER,

This is the second of five novellas on the women in the lineage of Jesus Christ. These were Eastern women who lived in ancient times, and yet their stories apply to our lives and the difficult issues we face in our world today. They were on the edge. They had courage. They took risks. They did the unexpected. They lived daring lives, and sometimes they made mistakes — big mistakes. These women were not perfect, and yet God in His infinite mercy used them in His perfect plan to bring forth the Christ, the Savior of the world.

We live in desperate, troubled times when millions seek answers. These women point the way. The lessons we can learn from them are as applicable today as when they lived thousands of years ago.

Tamar is a woman of **hope.**

Rahab is a woman of **faith.**

Ruth is a woman of **love.**

Bathsheba is a woman who received **unlimited grace.**

Mary is a woman of **obedience.**

These are historical women who actually lived. Their stories, as I have told them, are based on biblical accounts. Though some of their actions may seem disagreeable to us in our century, we need to consider these women in the context of their own times.

This is a work of historical fiction. The outline of the story is provided by the Bible, and I have started with the facts provided for us there. Building on that foundation, I have created action, dialogue, internal motivations, and in some cases, additional characters that I feel are consistent with the biblical record. I have attempted to remain true to the scriptural message in all points, adding only what is necessary to aid in our understanding of that message.

At the end of each novella, we have included a brief study section. The ultimate authority on people of the Bible is the Bible itself. I encourage you to read it for greater understanding. And I pray that as you read the Bible, you will become aware of the continuity, the consistency, and the confirmation of God's plan for the ages — a plan that includes you.

Francine Rivers

SETTING THE SCENE

The sons of Israel, the chosen people of God, took their families to Egypt to escape a famine in their homeland. One of the twelve brothers, Joseph, held a high position in the Egyptian government, and as a result, his large extended family were honored as special guests of Pharaoh himself.

But as the years passed and the Hebrews multiplied, they fell out of favor and were eventually enslaved by the Egyptians. It took the leadership of Moses — and a series of breathtaking miracles performed by God Himself — to deliver them. God was taking His people home, back to Canaan, the land He had promised would belong to His people forever.

On the verge of reclaiming their "Promised Land," the Israelites' faith in God failed. Fearing the power of the Canaanites, they refused to obey God's command to advance and take the land. Their disbelief and disobedience resulted in a forty-year delay in the fulfillment of God's promise. During those forty years, the Israelites wandered as nomads in the desert. All of the adults who had left Egypt — and rebelled against God — died in the wilderness.

Finally a new generation grew up, ready to take its place as God's army and claim the land promised to its ancestors. Of the original multitude that had left Egypt, only Moses and his two assistants, Joshua and Caleb, survived.

As the people of Israel approached the Promised Land for the second time, no one could stand against them. First the king of Arad, then King Sihon of the Amorites, then King Og of Bashan — all were put to the sword, their armies annihilated. In desperation, King Balak of Moab hired a sorcerer, Balaam, to curse the Israelites. To Balak's horror, God used Balaam to instead pronounce blessings upon His chosen people.

Finally, even the five kings of Midian together were unsuccessful in stopping the advancing Israelite army. Kings Evi, Rekem, Zur, Hur, and Reba all died in battle, their armies slaughtered, their towns and villages burned, their wealth seized as plunder.

The time had come. The people of God

were ready to claim their inheritance from God — the Promised Land. After designating Joshua as the new leader of Israel, the venerable Moses died, and the people prepared to cross the last remaining barrier between them and Canaan: the Jordan River, swollen with spring floods.

Now, all nations quake in terror at the knowledge that Israel is encamped at Shittim, just a short distance from Jericho. The walled fortress, the gateway to Canaan, awaits.

ONE

Rahab studied the distant plain of Jericho from her window in the city wall, her heart stirring with fear and excitement. Out there, just beyond the Jordan River, the Israelites were encamped, only the floodwaters holding them back. Soon they would cross over and come against the king of Jericho with the same ferocity they had shown in battle against Sihon, Og, and the five kings of Midian. And everyone in Jericho would die.

The king had doubled the guard at the gate and posted soldiers on the battlements. But it would do no good. Destruction was on the horizon. The only hope was to surrender and plead for mercy. The king worried about the size of the invading army, but he failed to see the real danger: the God of the Hebrews. All of Pharaoh's warriors hadn't been enough to defeat Him forty years ago. Not even the pantheon of gods and goddesses had saved Egypt. But all the king of Jericho could think about was improving the battlements, stockpiling weapons, and increasing the number of soldiers! Did men never learn?

Jericho was doomed!

And she was imprisoned inside the city, bound by a life she had carved out for herself years ago. What hope had she, a harlot? Her fate had been set in motion years ago, when she was little more than a child, a peasant's daughter summoned by a king.

"You must go!" her father had said. "As long as you live in the palace and please him, I shall prosper. He's arranging marriages for your sisters. And if you refuse, he will have you nonetheless, killing me to remove any obstacles. Think of the honor he bestows upon you. He chooses only the most beautiful girls, Rahab."

An *honor*? "And will he marry me, Father?" Her father couldn't look into her eyes. She knew the answer. The king had several wives, all of whom he had married for political advantages. She had nothing a king needed — merely a body he wanted to use.

Even then, young as she had been, she knew that lust burned hot but eventually turned to ashes. In a week, a month, a year

18

perhaps, the king would tire of her and send her home wearing a beautiful Babylonian robe and a few pieces of gold jewelry her father would confiscate and sell for his own profit.

"When I return, will you allow me to sell dates and pomegranates in the marketplace again, Father, or will I end up like so many others? Selling my body for a loaf of bread?"

He had covered his face and wept. She'd hated him for taking advantage of her ruin, hated him for making excuses, hated him for telling her she would be better off in the king's palace than in the grove hut where he and her mother and brothers and sisters lived. She hated him because he had no power to save her.

She had hated her own helplessness most of all.

Even in her wrath, Rahab had known her father couldn't save her from the king's lust. A king could take what he wanted. Any gifts he gave were meant to dissolve thoughts of revenge. Life was hard and uncertain, but if the right opportunity arose, a beautiful daughter could make a father's way smooth. Tax exemptions. Land use. An elevated position in the court. The king was generous when it served him, but usually his generosity lasted only as long as his lust.

Rahab rested her arms on the window, gazing out. She remembered setting foot in the palace that first day, vowing not to end up as a discarded sandal. She intended to find a way to take advantage of her wretched situation and the man who used her. She'd hidden her fury and revulsion, pretending to enjoy the king's embrace. Every moment in his company, her mind was crouched like a lioness studying its prey, watching, waiting for his weakness to show. And she found it soon enough: the constant arrival of emissaries, spies, and messengers. Without their stream of information, he wouldn't know who his enemies were or what petty jealousies and rebellions were on the rise.

"Give me a house, and I'll gather information for you," she had boldly proposed, once her opportunity became clear to her. How the king had laughed at her sagacity! She'd laughed with him, but continued to entice and solicit for further benefits. She was tenacious in her determination to have something tangible when she left the palace, something with which she could make her own way and sustain herself comfortably for a lifetime. She deserved it after suffering the caresses of that fat, foul-smelling, arrogant old man!

Well, she had gotten what she wanted: a

house, a prosperous living, and the illusion of independence. The king had given her this house situated near the eastern gate so she could watch the comings and goings of Jericho. For twelve years she'd looked out this window and picked out men to share her bed, men who might tell her things that would protect the king's throne and increase his treasury. Every transaction she made brought a double payment. The men paid to sleep with her, and the king paid for the grains of information she gleaned. She knew even more about what was happening outside the walls of Jericho than the king did. And when she wanted to know what was going on inside the palace, she beckoned Cabul, the captain of the guard. He could always be counted on to spill out every secret while in her arms.

She owned half a dozen Babylonian robes, boxes inlaid with bone and ivory and filled with jewelry. Her house was furnished with objects of art, her floor covered with multi-colored, woven rugs. Her customers slept on the finest colored linen sheets from Egypt perfumed with myrrh, aloe, and cinnamon. She could afford tasty delicacies and rich, heady wines. Everyone in the city knew she was a friend and confidante of the king. They also knew she was a whore.

But no one knew how much she hated her life. No one guessed how helpless she felt in the face of the plans made for her by father and king. Many would wonder why she had cause to complain. On the outside, she had an enviable life. The king respected her, men desired her, and she could choose her clientele. There were even women in Jericho who envied her independence. They didn't know what it felt like to be used, stripped of humanity. Even now, despite a house of her own and plush surroundings, she was helpless to change anything about her life. She was locked into it.

Yet no one knew the fierce heart that beat within her. No one suspected the stored resentment, the gathering fury, the aching hunger to break free and escape. She was in a prison others had made for her, a prison she had succeeded in filling with earthly treasures. But she had other plans, other dreams and hopes.

And they all depended on the God out there, the One she knew had the power to save those He chose. Somehow she had known — even as a young girl hearing the stories for the first time — that He was a true God, the only true One. When He brought His people across the Jordan, He would take this city and crush it as He had crushed all His enemies.

The end of everything she had known was in sight.

We're all going to die! Doesn't anyone else see that? Are they all blind and deaf to what's been happening for the last forty years? People come and go as they always have, thinking everything is going to be all right. They think the walls we've built will protect us, just as I thought the walls of my father's hut could protect me all those years ago. And we're not safe — we're not safe at all!

She was filled with the terror of death, filled even more with a terrible longing to be a part of what would come. She wanted to belong to the God who was coming. She felt like a little girl wanting desperately to be swept up in her father's arms and saved from destruction.

Several months ago, an Egyptian had spent a night telling her stories of the God of the Israelites. "But everyone says those are myths," she had said, wondering whether he believed the tales he repeated.

"Oh, no. My father was a boy when the plagues came. . . ." He'd talked far into the night about the signs and wonders and about a man named Moses. "He's dead now, but there's another . . . Joshua."

She went to the king the next morning,

but he was only interested in tactics, weaponry, numbers. "It's the *God* of the Hebrews you need to fear, my king," she said, but he waved her away impatiently.

"You disappoint me, Rahab, talking like a hysterical woman."

She wanted to shout at him. Moses might be a great leader, but no man could break the might of Egypt. Only a true God could do that! And He was out there, preparing His people to take all of Canaan.

But one look into the king's eyes and she knew pride was on the throne. Men listened only to what they wanted to hear.

Now, sitting at her window, she stretched her hands out and waved them. *Oh, how I wish I were one of Your people, for You alone are a true God.* Her eyes were hot and gritty. *I would bow down to You and give You offerings if given the chance!* She put her hands down and turned away. She could wish all she wanted, but she was going to share the same fate as everyone else trapped inside these walls. This fortress would become a slaughterhouse.

Because the king was stubborn and proud. Because the king thought the walls were high enough and thick enough to keep him safe. Because he was too stubborn and stupid to put his pride aside for the sake of his people. The king was afraid of the Israelites, but it was their God he should fear. She had known men all her life, and they were all much the same. But this God, He was different. She could *feel* His presence in some strange way she couldn't define, and she was filled with a sense of awe and urgency. Oh, how fortunate were those who belonged to Him! They had *nothing* to fear.

Although she had told the king everything she learned, he refused to listen. Still, she kept trying.

"I never knew you to be so fainthearted, my sweet. Those Hebrews will tuck tail and flee the same way they did forty years ago when the Amalekites joined forces with us. My father drove them out of the land. If they have such a mighty god on their side, why didn't they prevail against us then? Plagues . . . seas opening . . ." He sneered. "Myths to frighten us."

"Have you forgotten Sihon?"

He paled, his eyes narrowing coldly at her reminder. "No army can break through our walls."

"Before it's too late, send emissaries of peace with gifts for their God."

"What? Are you mad? Do you think our

priests would agree to that? We have gods of our own to appease! They've always protected us in the past. They'll protect us now."

"The same way Egypt's gods protected her? Egypt bows down to insects, and this God sent swarms to destroy their crops. They worship their Nile River, and this God turned it to blood."

"They're just stories, Rahab. Rumors to spread fear among our people. And you add to them! Go back to your house and do what you do best. Watch for foreign spies. . . ."

And so she did, but not for his sake.

Cabul talked freely last night, boasting of manpower, weapons, and the continuous sacrifices being made to the gods of Canaan. "We'll be fine. Don't worry your pretty head."

Fools! They were all fools! Surely the God who mocked the gods of Egypt and opened the Red Sea would find it easy to break down these walls! What good would stone and mortar idols do against a God who controlled wind, fire, and water? Rahab was certain that one breath from His lips would blow open the gates of Jericho. A sweep of His hand would make rubble of all the king's defenses!

But no one would listen.

So be it. She had given her last warning. Let it be on the king's head what happened to Jericho. She was going to find a way to align herself with those who would have the victory. If she didn't, she would die.

How could she get out of Jericho without jeopardizing the lives of her family members? If she left, the king would have her followed. She would be captured and executed for treason, and every member of her family would suffer the same fate to prevent the spread of her rebellion. No, she couldn't leave Jericho unless she took her father and mother and brothers and sisters and their families with her. But that would be impossible! Even if she could find a way to leave without arousing suspicion, her family wouldn't come. Her father believed whatever the king said. It wasn't in his nature to think for himself.

Rahab raked her fingers through her hair, pushing the curly dark mass over her shoulder. "Rahab!" someone called from below. She didn't look down. She wasn't interested in a merchant from Jebus or the owner of a caravan taking spices to Egypt or another soldier from a vanquished army. They were all walking dead. They just didn't know it yet. Only those Hebrews out there beyond the river were alive. For their God was no stone idol carved by human hands. He was the God of heaven and earth!

And I am just a rat inside a hole in this wall. . . .

What a strange and marvelous God He was! He had chosen the Hebrews — a nation of slaves — and set them free from Egypt, the most powerful nation on earth. He had taken the lowest of the low and used them to bring down the mighty. She'd heard that He'd even rained bread upon His people. They had nothing to fear, for He was mighty in deeds and yet showed kindness and mercy to them. Who would not love such a God?

Her king. Her people.

I would love Him! Her mouth trembled, and her eyes were hot with tears. *I would serve Him any way He asked. Given the chance, I would bow down before Him and rejoice to be counted among His people!*

Cabul snored loudly from the bed behind her, reminding her of his unwelcome presence. She pressed her palms over her ears and shut her eyes tightly, filled with self-disgust and anger. If she gave in to her feelings, she would shake the man awake and scream at him to get out of her house. He hadn't told her anything new last night.

Cabul was a waste of her time.

She watched the road again. She had one small glimmer of hope that had been roused by something her father had told her. Moses had sent spies into the land forty years ago. "We beat them back then." She had wondered about that, mulling over reasons for the Israelites' failure. They had been slaves, freed from mighty Egypt by an even mightier God. But perhaps they had still thought like slaves rather than men under the banner of a true God. Perhaps they had refused to obey. She could only guess why they had failed. But she knew it was not due to any failure of the God who rescued them.

Those who had rebelled all those years ago must surely be dead by now. A new generation had arisen, a generation who had been hardened by desert living, a generation who had been in the presence of Power from their birth. She could only hope that Joshua would do as Moses had done before him and send spies into the land. And she would have to be the first to spot them. With victory assured by their God, the Israelites didn't need to send anyone, but she still hoped the noble leader Joshua would take nothing for granted. Even if it wasn't necessary, it would be prudent to send spies to view the land and evaluate enemy defenses.

Please come. Please, please, please come. . . . I don't want to die. I don't want my family to die. Send someone. . . . Open my eyes so that I'll recognize them before the guards do. If they see them first and report to the king, all is lost!

"Rahab!" a man called to her again.

She glanced down impatiently and saw an Ishmaelite merchant waving at her from among the throng gathered at the gate. He was eager to lodge with her, but she spread her hands, shrugging and shaking her head. Let his camels keep him warm. He held up a gold necklace to bribe her. Ha! What good would gold do when the day of destruction came? "Give it to one of your wives!" she called back. Those around him laughed. Another man called up to her, but she ignored the entreaties and flatteries and watched the road.

Let them come to me.

If the spies were ragged from wandering, she would give them beautiful robes from Babylon. If they were thirsty, she would give them fine wine. If they were hungry, she would serve them a feast fit for kings. For they would come as servants of the Most High God. She would show them the honor meant for the One they served. For mighty was their God and worthy of tribute!

Her chest was tight with yearning. She wanted to be safe. As long as she was inside this wall, inside this city, she was condemned. She had to be counted among the Israelites to survive. The gods of the Jerichoans and Amorites and Perizzites and a dozen other tribes who inhabited Canaan wouldn't come to her rescue. They were stone tyrants with corrupt priests who demanded constant sacrifice. She'd seen babies taken from their mothers and placed on an altar, their little bodies boiled until the flesh fell away so the bones could be put into small bags and buried beneath the foundation of a new house or temple. As though murdered children could bring good fortune! She was thankful she had never had a child.

But if I did have one, I would give my baby to the God out there, the unseen One who dwells with His people, who shades them by day and keeps them warm at night, the One who protects those who belong to Him as though they were His children. A God like Him could be trusted. . . .

"Ah, the light." Cabul groaned. "Close the curtains!"

Rahab clenched her teeth; she kept her back to him. It was time the man was gone from her bed and her house. "The sun is up," she said in a pleasant voice. "Time you were as well."

She heard a muffled curse and the rustle of linen. "You're hard-hearted, Rahab."

She glanced at him over her shoulder and forced a sultry smile. "You didn't say that last night." She looked out the window again, searching, hoping to see someone who looked like an Israelite spy. What would one look like? How would she recognize one if he did come?

Cabul slid his arm around her waist and reached up to lift the curtain from the hook. "Come back to bed, my love." He pressed his lips to the curve of her neck.

She caught his hand before it could move to caress her. "The king will hear you're missing from your post. I wouldn't want to get you into trouble."

He laughed softly, his breath hot in her hair. "I won't be late."

She turned in his arms. "You must go, Cabul." She put her hands against his chest. "Your absence at the gate will be noticed, and I'll not have it said that Rahab caused a friend trouble."

"You are causing me pain right now."

"You're man enough to survive a small

discomfort."

He caught her hand as she moved away from him. "Is there a rich merchant below?"

"No."

"I heard someone calling your name."

"And what if you did?" Did he think putting a few coins in her hand meant he owned her? "You know what I do for a living."

He frowned, his eyes darkening.

Stifling her annoyance, she brushed her fingertips down his cheek and softened her tone. "Don't forget I came out of my house to find you." In her business, it was always wise to send a man away feeling he was someone special.

He grinned. "So you love me a little."

"Enough to wish you no harm." She allowed him to kiss her briefly and then disentangled herself. "A crowd is waiting at the gate, Cabul. It's time you opened it. If the merchants are annoyed, the king will hear about it." She crossed the room, leaned down, and swept up his clothes. Opening the door, she tossed them back at him. "You'd better hurry!" She laughed as she watched him dress hastily, then closed the door behind him. Dropping the bar to keep any would-be visitors out, she hurried back to her post at the window.

Solitude was a luxury. She stepped up and sat in the window, one leg dangling out. Ignoring the whistles from below, she watched the plain. Was that a column of smoke in the distance? She couldn't be sure. She had heard that the Israelites' God accompanied them as a column of smoke during the day and a pillar of fire at night.

When the heat became oppressive, she closed the curtains, left the window, and brushed her hair. She ate bread and sipped wine. But every few minutes, she parted the red-dyed linen and looked out again, studying every stranger who walked along the road.

Salmon had waited all his life to set foot in the Promised Land. He could see it from where he was camped. He was eager for the battles ahead, his confidence strengthened by past victories the Lord had given His people. It was the waiting that was difficult. Salmon felt like a horse reined in, prancing, champing at the bit, ready for the race to begin. He laughed, excitement coursing through him as he sparred with his friend Ephraim. It was early, the sun just rising, but every day was an opportunity to train, to prepare for God's work of taking the Promised Land.

Gripping his staff, he made a thrust. Ephraim parried, turned, and struck, but Salmon countered him. *Crack! Crack! Crack!* Ephraim came at him with fierce determination, but Salmon was ready. Turning, he swept the staff in a hard circle and swept Ephraim off his feet. Salmon was too confident, for he didn't expect Ephraim to make another swing at him from the ground, which landed Salmon on his back in the dust. Both lay in the dust, panting and grinning.

As soon as Salmon got his breath back, he laughed. "I'll be less smug next time."

"When do you think we'll attack Jericho?" Ephraim said, rising and dusting himself off.

Salmon sat up and looked toward the rise where Joshua stood each day, praying. "The Lord will tell Joshua when the time is right."

"I hope it's soon! Somehow the waiting is harder than the battle itself."

Salmon stood, his staff gripped in his hand. The desert wind stirred Joshua's robes as he stood on the rise. Since Moses had died, Salmon had turned his full attention to Joshua and Eleazar, the priest, for leadership. Whatever they said was law, for they followed the Lord wholeheartedly and spoke only what God instructed them to say. As a boy at his father's knee, Salmon had heard the story of how Joshua and Caleb had spied out the Promised Land and said it could be taken. They'd believed God's promise to give them the land, but the other ten spies had convinced the people — even the great leader Moses himself — that victory was impossible. The people had lacked faith and lost their opportunity, so the promise was deferred to the next generation. Salmon's generation. Salmon hadn't even been born when the Lord had passed judgment and sent the people back into the desert, but he'd been affected by it. He had grown up in the shadow of his father's shame and regrets.

How many times had he heard his father weeping? *"If only we'd listened. If only we'd believed Joshua and Caleb."* Over and over again, year after year. If whining could wear down the Lord, his father's surely would have. *"If only we'd listened, we wouldn't be out in this wilderness, wandering like lost sheep."* Salmon grimaced at the memory of his father's complaints and self-pity, for they hinted of the old rebellion and the unchanged attitude of a man's heart.

Lord God of mercy, save me from such thinking, he prayed. *Make me the man You want me to be — a man of courage, a man willing to step out immediately when You say go.*

It was too easy to sneer at the mistakes of others. Such arrogance. Salmon knew he was no better than the man who had fathered him. The danger was in looking too far ahead. He must *wait,* as Joshua was waiting. The Lord would speak when He was ready, and when God did speak, Salmon knew the choice would be presented to him: obey or disobey. He didn't want to hesitate like his father had. Better to fear God than men. No matter how frightened he might be of the battle ahead, he knew it was a more fearful thing to displease the Lord. Therefore, he set his mind on obedience. He wouldn't allow himself to give in to his human weaknesses, his fears. How could one fear men and please God?

Jehovah had promised the land of Canaan to His people. The day would come when He would call them to take hold of that promise. It would be up to Salmon and all those of his generation to obey.

So far, none had weakened, but a few were grumbling at the delay, and a few questioned.

Lord God of heaven and earth, I beg You to give me the confidence of Joshua. Instill in me Your purpose. Do not let me weaken. You are God and there is no other!

"Prepare yourself," Ephraim said.

Turning, Salmon brought his staff up and blocked Ephraim's blow.

When the Lord called him into battle, Salmon intended to be ready.

"Salmon."

He recognized the deep voice immediately. Jumping to his feet, he pulled back the tent flap and gaped at Joshua.

"I have work for you," the elderly man said calmly.

"Please, enter." Salmon stepped back quickly and bid his commander welcome.

The old warrior ducked his head slightly and entered the tent, looked around briefly, and faced Salmon once more. Salmon shook inwardly with excitement, for what greater honor could there be than to have Joshua seek him out? "Please sit here, sir." He offered him the most comfortable place.

Joshua inclined his head. Setting the bundle he had brought with him to one side, he folded his legs beneath him as easily as a young man. When he looked up at Sal-mon, his eyes were dark and intent, ablaze with purpose.

Under normal circumstances, the commander would have summoned him rather than come to his tent. "What can I serve you, sir?" Salmon said, curbing his curiosity in order to show respect and hospitality. Joshua would explain when he was ready.

Smiling slightly, Joshua held out his hand. "Nothing. But you can sit."

Salmon did so. Leaning forward, he clasped his hands and said nothing. The old man closed his eyes for a long moment and then raised his head and looked at him. "I need two men to go on a mission of great risk."

"I'll go." Salmon straightened, heart pounding. "Send me."

Joshua tipped his head to one side and considered him in amusement. "It might be prudent to hear what the mission is before you volunteer."

"If you want it done, it needs doing, and that's all I need to know. The Lord speaks through you. To obey you is to obey God. I'll go wherever you want me to go and do whatever you need done."

Joshua's eyes glowed. He leaned forward. "Then here are your instructions. Spy out the land on the other side of the Jordan River, especially around Jericho. See what defenses they have in place. Discern the mood of the people."

Fear caught Salmon unaware, but he set his mind against it. "When do you want me to leave?"

"Within the hour. Caleb is giving instructions to Ephraim." Joshua raised his hand. "I can see you're ready to grab your sword and go now, but hear me out. Other than Caleb and Ephraim, no one knows you're leaving camp. You'll be going in secret. You're young and on fire, my son, but you must be coolheaded and wise as a serpent. Do not stroll into the city like a conqueror. Keep your head down. Seek out an establishment that will know the mind of the people. Blend in. Keep your eyes and ears open. The battlements aren't as important as what the Jerichoans are thinking. Find out everything you can, and then get out of there as quickly as possible. Waste no time. Do you understand?"

"Yes, commander."

Joshua took the bundle he'd set aside and placed it between them. "Amorite clothing and a weapon."

The clothing had undoubtedly been taken from the body of a vanquished foe, for Salmon saw a stain of blood. He knew he would have to be careful when wearing the tunic. It would be difficult for him to blend in naturally among Jerichoans if anyone saw that stain. Anyone looking at it would know the last man who wore the garment had died a violent death. He would have to wear a mantle to cover it.

Joshua rose. Salmon sprang to his feet. Joshua turned before going out, put his hand on Salmon's shoulder, and gripped him strongly. "May the Lord watch over you and keep you safe!"

"Blessed be the name of the Lord."

Releasing him, Joshua swept the tent flap aside, stooped, and went out. Salmon held the flap open long enough to watch Joshua disappear among the other tents of Israel. Letting it drop back into place, he let out his breath sharply and dropped to his knees. Throwing back his head, Salmon closed his eyes and raised his hands, thanking God for this opportunity to serve. Then he prostrated himself and prayed for the wisdom and courage to complete the task.

By moonlight, Salmon and Ephraim girded their loins by drawing up the backs of their tunics and tucking them into their belts. Thus unencumbered, they ran, reaching the eastern bank of the Jordan well before daybreak. Gasping for breath, Salmon dumped his bundle on the ground, grasped his tunic, and hauled it up over his head.

"The river looks swift," Ephraim said, stripping off his clothing and catching the Amorite tunic Salmon tossed him.

Swollen by spring floods, the river rose over its banks. And Ephraim was right — the current was swift.

Salmon shrugged into the Amorite tunic. He nodded toward a sloping bank as he strapped on a leather belt. "We'll go in down there and start swimming."

Ephraim's mouth curved sardonically. "I hate to mention this now, friend, but I don't know how to swim."

Salmon laughed mirthlessly. "And you think I do? The desert hasn't exactly afforded us much opportunity to learn, has it?"

"So what are we going to do?"

"Cross over. Stop worrying. If God wills, we'll make it."

"And if not, we'll drown," Ephraim said flatly.

"Do you think the Lord has brought us this far to let us be defeated?"

Ephraim watched the river. "I'd feel better if I had a tree trunk to hang on to."

"The Lord will uphold us." Salmon spoke with more conviction than he felt. *Give me courage, Lord.* "Fill your lungs with air, keep your arms outstretched, and kick like a frog.

The current will carry us."

"All the way to the Salt Sea."

Salmon ignored his friend's grim sense of humor and pointed. "Aim for those willows on the other side." Tying the sheath to his belt, he jammed his dagger into it. "Let's go."

Despite his bravado, fear shot through Salmon as the river's current tugged hard at his legs. Overcoming his fear, he waded into the Jordan until the water was to his waist. Perhaps he could make it this way, one step at a time, using his own physical strength to keep himself on his feet. But the next step proved he couldn't. He slipped on some slick rocks and lost his footing. Panic gripped him as he was sucked into the current. He was pulled under briefly, but he fought his way up long enough to fill his lungs with air. His body rolled and turned, spun back. He hit something hard and almost lost his breath. Salmon fought his fear and the river, as the spring flood carried him along.

Lord, help me!

He saw the trees and kicked hard. Clawing the water, he used the current to steer his body. He kept his neck arched and stiff so that his head was above the water and he could breathe and see where he was going.

He heard a shout behind him but didn't have time to turn and see if Ephraim was doing any better than he. Making a lunge for an overhanging branch, he caught hold. Reaching up, he got a better grip and looked back. Ephraim was still standing on the far bank.

"Come on!" Salmon called to him.

Ephraim entered the river with obvious uneasiness. Stretching out his arms, he went in face first. Seeing how fast Ephraim was swept along, Salmon stretched out his body as far as possible so that his friend could reach his ankle. "Grab hold!"

Ephraim succeeded, but the jolt almost yanked Salmon free. His body swung hard around and jerked against the strong pull of the river. Water rippled violently over Ephraim's head. Clinging to the branch with one hand, Salmon reached down and grasped Ephraim and pulled. "Climb!" Ephraim reached up, his fingers biting into Salmon's thigh. Pulling himself higher, his head emerged from the rushing water. He gasped for breath. Salmon grabbed Ephraim's belt and hauled him up farther. Salmon shoved him toward the west bank.

When he made it to shore, Ephraim reached out and gave Salmon a hand and threw himself back as far as he could before the limb broke and toppled into the water. Gaining his footing in the rocky bottom, Salmon slogged his way out of the Jordan and collapsed to his knees. Ephraim was coughing violently.

Chest heaving, Salmon drank in the air. He dug his fingers into the soil and held it up to breathe in the scent of its richness. "The Lord has brought us over," he said in a voice choked with emotion. They were the first of their generation to set foot in the Promised Land. "The Lord be praised!"

Ephraim was still coughing up murky river water, but he managed to rasp, "May God grant we live long enough to enjoy it."

"Amen." Salmon rose. "It won't be long until daybreak." He was eager for the mission ahead, anxious to be on the move, but it wouldn't be wise to arrive wet and muddy from the river — or too early in the day, making them appear anxious to enter the city. Hunkering down by the Jordan, he washed. "If we hurry, we can make it to the palms before full daylight."

"Just give me a few minutes to rest, will you?"

"We've no time to waste. Rest while we walk!"

As they crossed the arid stretch of land west of the Jordan and gained the road, the sun rose behind them. Even from a distance of several miles, the lush green spring-fed oasis was visible, as were the high, thick walls of the City of Palms that blocked entrance into Canaan. Salmon's heart sank. These walls were so immense, they would be insurmountable by frontal attack. Nor could they be taken from the west, for behind the walled city was a towering backbone of steep, jagged mountains. "The city is well situated."

"And impregnable. How will we ever conquer such a city? Never has there been such a stronghold!"

Speechless, Salmon studied the walls. They were at least six times the height of any man, and there were battlements on both sides of the gate. Guards standing watch would see an army coming from miles away, giving them plenty of time to close the gates and prepare for battle.

Would Joshua have them build ladders to scale these walls? How many would die in setting them up and keeping them in place until enough soldiers could get over the wall? Could those immense gates be smashed or burned? How many would die in the battle for this city? Thousands! Would he be one of them — if he didn't die here today, on this mission?

"May God protect us from such an end," Salmon said under his breath.

"What should we do now?" Ephraim said. "Join the throng waiting for the gates to open?"

"We'll wait until late in the day. Better if we aren't inspected too closely. The guards will be less attentive then."

They found a grassy place not far from a spring-fed stream and slept in the shade of the City of Palms.

Two

At first glance, Rahab dismissed the two men as Amorite soldiers carrying a message to the king. But as they came closer, she noticed their interest in the walls. The men, who carried no packs or parcels, seemed grim as they spoke to one another, watchful of the guard towers. Even more telling was their complete disinterest in her. Soldiers, even those on a serious mission, invariably looked for women of her calling. They were always eager for a comfortable night's lodging, food, drink, and fleshly pleasures whenever they could get them. Amorite soldiers were especially lustful and profane.

Ah, the men had spotted her. "Hello, my fine friends!" she called, smiling and waving. They turned their faces away. Odd. They were young, but not so young they should be embarrassed by a woman's attentions.

Or had that been disgust on their faces?

An uncomfortable feeling curled in the pit of her stomach. It had been years since she had felt shame or the desire to cover her face and hide. Not since the first few weeks she had been in the king's company. No matter what her father had said, she knew in her heart that what was being done to her was wrong, and for her to take advantage of it was even worse. It had been a confusing time, a time of degradation and elevation. But no one had dared openly look down upon a young woman chosen by the king. She had been treated with deference during her months in the palace. And with time, she had learned to hide her feelings. She had learned to hold her head up and walk like a queen, even though every prospect of having an honorable future had been stripped from her.

In spite of her discomfort — or perhaps even because of it — her interest in the two men increased. She was certain they were not what they appeared to be. True Amorite soldiers would strut and swagger. They would call out lewd suggestions to her and make offers of money. They would boast of their prowess with women.

Were these the Israelite spies she'd hoped would come?

The desert wind came up, swirling dust

around the two. The outer garment on the taller man blew open. He snatched the garment closed. But not before she saw the stain he'd quickly hidden.

Her heart leapt. Rahab drew in her breath sharply and leaned forward. She was determined now to gain their attention. No matter how brazen she had to be, she would make them look up at her. She leaned so far out the window that her black curling hair spilled like a dark waterfall against the stone. "You, there!" she shouted. "You two!"

The taller man glanced up, and his face went red. She waved. "I want to welcome you!"

"We're not interested!"

Clearly, he was displeased with her continued attention. He muttered something to his companion and kept walking.

She wasn't about to give up, no matter how contemptuous he was of her. "I can't remember the last time a man tried so hard to ignore me!"

Irritated, he stopped. "We haven't enough money for your services."

"Have I set a price?"

He gave a dismissive wave, jerked his head at his companion, who was gawking at her, and strode on.

When had she ever had to talk a man into

spending time with her? If she leaned out her window any farther, she'd fall at his feet! "I have cool wine, fresh bread, and a comfortable place for you both to sleep." When they still ignored her, she tore off her slipper and threw it at them. "Most Amorites call out my name when they approach the gate!" She'd always been the one to ignore them, unless the soldier happened to be a commander and held information of interest to the king. Normally she would not have given these ordinary soldiers a second glance, but they were Israelite spies. She knew it. Clearly, they saw her as nothing more than a common harlot plying her trade.

Fear swept through her for their sake. Did they think the guards posted at the gates were fools and wouldn't see through their disguise? She must get their attention quickly. One look at these wary fellows and the guards would be on top of them, swords drawn. By tomorrow morning, their heads would be lopped off and their bodies tied to the wall!

"Even the king has drunk wine from my cup and eaten bread from my hand!"

The taller one stopped and looked up at her again. "Why do you honor us with your attention?"

51

His mockery stung, but she swallowed her pride and answered plainly. "Because I have wisdom beyond my years, young man, wisdom I can share with you if you're wise enough to listen." She kept her tone teasingly seductive, for they were close enough to the gate that one of the guards might take note of the conversation. "I know what you want."

"Oh, do you?"

Save her from self-righteous, callow youth! "Every man needs to eat and rest." If he turned away again, she would throw a jug at him. "And a few come for intelligent conversation." She noted the sudden tension in his body. Just to be sure he understood her, she smiled. "The Jordan is high this time of year, isn't it?" She raised her brows and said nothing more.

Perhaps she had gone too far, for never had she seen a fiercer look.

"We are tired and hungry," he conceded.

"You will be glad you tarried with me."

"How do we find you?"

"I'll meet you inside the gate and show you the way." She blew them a kiss for the sake of the guard who had taken a sudden interest. She was shaking with excitement as she stepped down off the stool and yanked the cord holding the curtain back.

Raking her fingers through her hair, she braided it quickly before hurrying out.

Rahab raced down the steps and around the corner. It was the hottest time of day. Few people were on the walkway that ran along the inside of the city wall. Many had worked during the morning hours and were now resting. When she entered the gate, she saw that Cabul had noticed the men. Slowing her pace, she sauntered closer, leaning against the cold stone. "Cabul!"

He turned and grinned, then left his post and came to her. "What brings you out so late in the day, my beauty?"

"You, of course." She kept her tone light and teasing.

He laughed. "More likely a wealthy merchant or an emissary from the Philistines."

She raised her brows and gave him a shrewd look. "One never knows."

Chuckling softly, he took her hand. His eyes narrowed. "You're shaking."

"Too much wine last night." She moved closer, toying with the hilt of his sword while looking past him. The two men were entering the gate.

"You weren't drinking with me," Cabul said and tipped her chin. "What do you say I come up after I get off duty and we'll get drunk together?"

"I think I'll forgo wine for a few days."

"Then we could —"

She slapped his arm playfully. No one was challenging the two strangers. Several city elders were arguing among themselves, and the soldier who'd taken Cabul's post seemed more interested in them than in two young Amorites dusty from travel.

"Did you come down here just to tease me?"

"Never." She raised her head again, gazing into Cabul's eyes. "You know I think you're the most handsome fellow in the king's service." And he was arrogant enough to believe her.

Cabul grinned and started to say something when two elders started shouting angrily at one another. Glancing back, he spotted the two strangers. When the taller young man looked her way, Cabul frowned. "Amorite soldiers? I never thought you'd stoop that low."

She shrugged. "Who knows? They may have news that will be of interest to the king."

Troubled, he looked at them again. "These are dangerous times, Rahab. They could be spies."

Her pulse rocked. "Do you think so?"

"Their hair is too short."

"Maybe they've taken some kind of vow." She touched his arm and smiled up at him. "I must say I'm touched you're so concerned for my welfare, but let me conduct my own business. The king wouldn't appreciate your interference in my affairs. If they are spies, he'll want to know about it."

"Are you about the king's interests, Rahab?"

She glared at him purposely. "What do you think?"

"Be careful, then. Israelites show no mercy, even to women and children." His dark eyes were filled with fear, but not on her behalf. "I'll tell the king."

"Wait a while. You don't want them to leave before we can find out why they've come." She knew him well enough to sense his tension. He was silent for a moment, undoubtedly calculating what would please the king most. She planted a suggestion. "Give me time with them, Cabul. They'll be easier to take if I fill them with good wine."

"You may be right."

"Of course I'm right." She toyed with his tunic. "Besides, I know the king better than you." She looked up at him through her lashes. "These men could bring me a fat pouch of gold, and if you allow me more than an hour with them, I'll give a portion to you."

His jaw clenched and unclenched. She knew his greed warred with his sense of duty. Would his desire for money outweigh his fear of failing to report immediately to the king? "I'll give you as much time as I can," he concluded.

When Cabul walked away, she looked at the two men trying so hard to appear inconspicuous among the bustling Jericho-ans bargaining in the gate. She motioned to them. Perhaps they hesitated now because they'd seen her speaking with Cabul and thought she was setting a trap.

Cabul was watching them. He glanced at her and jerked his chin. Go on, he was saying. Take advantage of the opportunity. She could imagine what he was thinking. Better she risk her life than he risk his. So be it!

Smiling boldly, she strolled over to the two men. "Welcome to Jericho."

Salmon followed the woman along the walkway. He'd thought her disturbingly beautiful even from a distance, but close up, she took his breath away. He hadn't expected to face any kind of temptation on this mission, but he was having a hard time keeping his eyes off her hips and his mind on his business. How old was she? Thirty? Thirty-five? Her body didn't show it, but her eyes did.

She opened a door and entered quickly, standing just inside and beckoning them impatiently.

Salmon entered first, Ephraim following.

"Look at this place," Ephraim muttered under his breath as he stood, gaping, in the middle of the room. Salmon glanced around at the carpets, cushions in all colors, and red curtains held back by thick crimson cords. He tried not to look at the bed that dominated the room. The air held the fragrance of incense and cinnamon. He looked around. Evidently her profession paid well.

Closing the door behind them, the woman threw off her shawl. "I've got to hide you!"

"What are you talking about, woman?"

"Don't pretend ignorance. You're Israelite spies. If it wasn't written all over you before, it is now." She went for the ladder against the back wall.

Ephraim looked at Salmon. "What do we do?"

Salmon stared at her. "How did you know?"

She rolled her eyes and shook her head.

"You mean aside from the way you studied the walls and battlements?" She dragged the ladder across the room. "There's a bloodstain on your tunic. I imagine the man who wore it before you died in it."

Salmon blocked her way. For one brief instant, he considered killing her so he could complete his mission. She lifted her head and straightened, her brown eyes clear and intelligent. "The soldier you saw speaking to me? He knows who you are."

"You told him?"

"He guessed." She grew impatient. "You came for information, didn't you? It would be better if you lived long enough to get it." She thrust the ladder at him and pointed at the hatch door to the roof. "Hurry! What're you waiting for? The king's executioner?"

Ephraim protested. "The roof is the first place the soldiers will look!"

"They won't have to look if you're still standing in the middle of the room!"

Ephraim looked around. "There must be a better place!"

"Fine." The woman put her hands on her hips. "If you don't like the roof, how about my bed?"

Horrified, Ephraim went up the ladder.

Her expression became pained as she watched Ephraim's hasty retreat. "I thought he'd feel that way." She looked at Salmon. He thought she had the most beautiful dark brown eyes he'd ever seen. No wonder Joshua and Caleb had given so many warnings about foreign women. "Now, how about you?" she said, her mouth tipped ruefully.

Salmon put his foot on the bottom rung, then looked at her again. "What's your name?"

"Rahab, but we haven't time to talk now. *Move!*"

She followed him up the ladder. Pushing him, she gestured to Ephraim. "Lie down over there, and I'll cover you both with the bundles of flax."

Salmon did as she instructed and watched her as she worked with quick efficiency, stacking the bundles carefully over them. Finishing the task, she leaned down and whispered, "I'm sorry I'm unable to make you more comfortable, but please be still until I return." She hurried back to the ladder, pulling the hatch over the opening as she went down.

"We're putting our lives into the hands of a harlot!" Ephraim said in a hoarse whisper.

"Have you got any better ideas?"

"I wish we had our swords!"

"It's a good thing we didn't, or we'd be in

the hands of that guard at the gate who spoke with Rahab."

"Rahab? You asked her name?"

"It seemed appropriate under the circumstances."

"What makes her important?" Ephraim said. "You know what she is." His tone dripped with contempt.

"Keep your voice down!"

"Should we huddle under these bundles of flax like cowards? Better if we kill her now and get about our business."

Salmon caught hold of Ephraim before he could throw the bundles off. "Better if we finish what we were sent to do! Or have you forgotten the mission Joshua assigned us: get into the city, get information, get out! He didn't say to shed any blood." He released his friend. "Who better to know the pulse of Jericho than a whore who's broken bread with the king?"

"I'd rather die by the sword than be caught hiding behind a woman's skirts."

"We're not hiding behind her skirts," Salmon said with some amusement. "We're hiding under her bundles of flax."

"How can you laugh? We have only her word about the king. Why should we trust the word of a harlot?"

"Didn't you look at her?"

"Not as closely as you did."

"She's beautiful enough to attract a king's attention."

"Perhaps, but did you see how familiar that guard was with her? She's probably broken bread with every man in the city and hundreds who've come to trade, besides."

"Then she'll know the pulse of the city."

"And probably have every disease known to man."

"Be quiet! We're where God has placed us." Salmon wondered why his friend's words had roused such anger in him. Rahab was probably everything Ephraim said she was. So why this strong desire to defend her? And why was he trusting her with their lives?

He let out his breath, forcing himself to relax. "We'd better rest while we can. I have the feeling, one way or another, we won't be inside these walls for long."

Rahab knew the king's men would come soon. The moment she departed the gate with the two Israelites, Cabul would have run to his commander to give a report on the two strangers who'd entered the city.

She descended the ladder, grasped it, and swung it down.

"Rahab! Open up!"

Pulse jumping, she ran her hands over her face to wipe away any perspiration. Patting her hair and straightening her dress, she went quickly to the door and opened it wide, pretending relief at the sight of the men standing outside. "I wish you'd come sooner, Cabul."

Flushed and tense, Cabul remained where he was standing. Other soldiers were behind him, armed and ready for a fight. She could see the fear in their eyes, a fear that matched her own, though for different reasons. If Cabul conducted himself properly, he would enter her house and make a complete search, including the roof. And if he found the spies, she was a dead woman.

"The king's orders are that you bring out the men who have come into your house. They are spies sent here to discover the best way to attack us." His gaze darted past her. "Produce them."

"The men were here earlier, but I didn't know where they were from. They left the city at dusk, as the city gates were about to close, and I don't know where they went. If you hurry, you can probably catch up with them."

"Where did they go?"

"I don't know," she repeated. Cabul would

have more to face now than two spies. He would have to answer to a frightened, angry king for failing to take them into custody. "Quick! Go after them. You still have time to overtake them if you hurry!"

He didn't question her. Why should he suspect her of treason when she had proven herself loyal to the king so many times? Hadn't she made a prosperous living gleaning information from strangers so that she could report to the king and receive a reward? Her word was enough to send him on his way. Turning on his heel, Cabul shouted orders and headed straight for the gate.

Rahab stepped out of her house and watched them depart in the deepening twilight. As soon as they rounded the corner, she went back into her house, closed the door, locked it, and ran to her window. Her palms were sweating, her heart pounding wildly. By now, Cabul and the others were at the gate. She could hear him shouting for the guards on duty to open it so they could pursue the spies. If Cabul paused long enough to speak with the men on duty, he might learn that the men fitting the strangers' description had not left the city.

She breathed easier when she saw Cabul appear outside the wall. The others followed him as they hurried away from the city. They were heading east for the Jordan, running now, spears in their hands, certain they could overtake the spies before they crossed the river. And the gate was closed behind them.

Rahab shut her eyes and smiled. She waited several more minutes to be sure Cabul and the others were far enough away. Then she gathered a jug of wine, bread, and a basket of dates and pomegranates and dragged out the ladder to set it up once more.

The men on the roof were silent. Could they have fallen asleep? Setting down the food she had brought with her, she crossed the roof quietly, took up a bundle of flax, and set it aside. She didn't want to startle them.

"The soldiers are gone now. It's safe to come out."

The taller man sat up first. When he looked at her, she felt the impact of his gaze. He was curious about her, and he was disturbed by his attraction to her. He said nothing as his companion stood up and brushed himself off. "We heard shouting."

She wanted to put them at ease. "The soldiers have left the city in pursuit of you." When she stretched out her hand, she realized she was shaking badly enough for them to notice. "I have bread and wine."

She understood their hesitation. She was a Jerichoan and a harlot. Why should they trust her? They must be wondering why a Canaanite would protect them. They might even wonder how she'd managed to get rid of the soldiers so quickly, without their even searching the house. Why should these Israelites believe anything a harlot had to say? But believe her they must. So many lives depended on it.

Rahab lowered her hand and lifted her chin. "I know the Lord has given you this land," she told them. "We are all afraid of you. Everyone is living in terror. For we have heard how the Lord made a dry path for you through the Red Sea when you left Egypt. And we know what you did to Sihon and Og, the two Amorite kings east of the Jordan River, whose people you completely destroyed. No wonder our hearts have melted in fear!"

She wondered why they'd even come here. Surely they knew better than she that the land was theirs! Why should they come to spy out a land the Lord had already given them? Did they doubt? Did they need encouragement?

"No one has the courage to fight after

65

hearing such things. For the Lord your God is the supreme God of the heavens above and the earth below." Her eyes filled with tears, for her heart ached deeply to be counted among the chosen people of this God.

Swallowing hard, she stepped forward and spread her hands. "Now swear to me by the Lord that you will be kind to me and my family since I have helped you. Give me some guarantee that when Jericho is conquered, you will let me live, along with my father and mother, my brothers and sisters, and all their families."

The taller man glanced at his companion, who stared at Rahab. There was enough moonlight that she could see his consternation. The taller man looked at her again, his expression curiously excited. "My name is Salmon, and this is Ephraim. We offer our own lives as a guarantee for your safety."

Her heart soared with relief and thanksgiving. She looked at the other for his response.

"I agree," Ephraim said with less enthusiasm, giving Salmon a disgruntled look. He looked at her again. "If you don't betray us, we will keep our promise when the Lord gives us the land."

She smiled broadly, elated. She would trust these men with her life and the lives of those she loved. She had made them swear to her by the Lord. They wouldn't dare break such an oath. The faith they had in their mighty God would make them uphold it.

"Please," she said, extending her hand toward the cushions in one corner of the flat roof. "Sit. Make yourselves comfortable. You're my guests." She busied herself with the food she had brought with her. "What can I serve you? I have dates, almonds, honey and raisin cakes, bread, wine . . ."

"Nothing," Ephraim said coldly.

"But thank you," Salmon added, as if to ease the rejection.

Rahab turned and studied them. Though they had promised to save her life and the lives of her family members, it seemed all too clear they wanted no part of her. Especially the man called Ephraim. He made her feel like a bug that had crawled out from under a rock. The other young man studied her with open curiosity. She sat down on a cushion and looked at him. "Ask whatever you want."

He looked into her eyes intently. "How did you come by your faith in our God?"

"I've heard stories about Him since I was a girl."

"So has everyone else in Jericho."

She blinked. "I know that all too well, and I can't explain why I believed when everyone else didn't."

"Your people are afraid," Ephraim said. "We heard enough at the gate to know that much."

"Yes, they're afraid of you, as they would be any conquering army. But they don't understand that it is your God who gives you victory."

Salmon's eyes shone as he studied her face. Then his eyes moved down over her and back up again as though taking her in all at once. She could see plainly enough that he liked what he saw. So did she. He was a very handsome young man.

Ephraim seemed determined to keep her in her place. "You have gods of your own."

"Wooden statues of no earthly use," she said disdainfully. "Did you see any in my chamber?" Ephraim looked uncomfortable. "Go on down," she said, gesturing toward the ladder. "Open the cabinets. Look behind the curtains, under the bed. Search anywhere you wish, Ephraim. You will not find any idols or talismans among my possessions. I lost faith in the gods of my people long ago."

"Why?"

The Hebrew seemed intent upon testing her. So be it. She was more than willing to comply. "Because they couldn't save me. They're just things made by men, and I know how weak men are." She spread her hands in a gesture of appeal. "I want to live among your people."

Ephraim frowned slightly and looked at Salmon.

Salmon leaned forward slightly. "You must understand that we have laws, laws given to us by God Himself."

"I would like to know these laws." She had felt some message pass between the two men and sensed it would affect her greatly.

Salmon considered her for a moment and then said quietly, "There are laws against fornication and adultery."

Ephraim was not so gentle in his condemnation of her profession. "Prostitution is not tolerated. Anyone found practicing it is executed."

Rahab remembered how she had hung out her window and called down to them as she had a hundred others before them. The heat poured into her face. Never had she felt such self-loathing. No wonder they had hesitated. No wonder they wouldn't eat food from her table or drink so much as a drop of water. She was filled with shame.

"I didn't choose this lifestyle," she said in quick defense. "I was presented to the king by my father when I was a girl and had no say —" She stopped when she saw Salmon's grimace. What did it matter how she had come to be what she was? She had sensed from the beginning that it was wrong. What did it matter that she had been just a girl and had to do what she was told? Did that excuse continuing in her profession these past years and gaining wealth from it? No! She frowned and looked away, feeling the Hebrews' perusal. She looked at them again, calm and accepting. "If God loathes prostitution, then I'm done with it."

Salmon rose and walked to the edge of the roof. He stared out across the city for a long moment and then turned and looked at her again. "It's time for us to leave," he said. "We've served our purpose in coming, Ephraim."

Rahab rose abruptly. She knew they had to act quickly now. She hurried down the ladder into the house, followed by the two men. Crossing the room, she untied and yanked free the crimson rope that held her curtains back from her bed. "You can't go by way of the gate. I can lower you from the window with this." Looping it up, she went to the window, brushed Salmon aside, and dropped one end over the sill. She peered out as the crimson cord snaked down the wall. "It reaches to within ten feet of the ground."

"Close enough." Salmon took the rope from her hand and set her aside. "You first," he said, nodding to his friend. Ephraim lifted himself up and swung his legs out the window.

"Wait!" Rahab said. "Escape to the hill country," she told them. "Hide there for three days until the men who are searching for you have returned; then go on your way."

Ephraim nodded, grasped the rope, and went out the window. Rahab heard a soft cascade of loosened mortar, then a thud as he hit the ground. Salmon handed the rope to her and sat on the windowsill.

"Listen to me, Rahab. We can guarantee your safety only if you leave this scarlet rope hanging from the window. And all your family members — your father, mother, brothers, and all your relatives — must be here inside the house. If they go out into the street, they will be killed, and we cannot be held to our oath. But we swear that no one inside this house will be killed — not a hand will be laid on any of them."

She bit her lip as gratitude filled her.

He swung one leg out and looked back at her. "If you betray us, however, we are not bound by this oath in any way."

"I accept your terms," she replied.

The look in his eyes changed subtly. Letting go of the rope, he reached out and cupped the back of her head, pulling her close. Her heart stopped, for she thought he meant to kiss her.

"Don't be afraid. I'll be back for you."

"I hope so."

He released her and took up the rope. "Are you strong enough to hold me?"

She laughed. "I'll have to be!" She held on with all her strength, and when she thought she'd fail, she found strength she didn't know she had.

When Salmon let go of the rope, she stood on her tiptoes and looked out the window. Both men stood below her. Ephraim was looking around cautiously, but Salmon grinned up at her. He raised his hand in a gesture of salutation and promise. She waved for him to go quickly.

She smiled when she saw they took the road leading to the hill country.

THREE

Salmon and Ephraim followed the road over the mountains into the hill country. It was well past dawn when they rested near a small stream. Kneeling, eyes alert, they drank and drank their fill.

Ephraim trapped several fish in a pool and flipped them onto the bank, where Salmon had built a small fire. After cleaning them, Salmon roasted the fish on a stick. Salmon had never eaten anything but manna and found the fish a new and interesting taste to his palate. Replete, they saw a Canaanite shepherd bring his flock of goats to drink downstream. The man glanced their way, then drove his flock west.

"He's afraid of strangers," Ephraim said.

"The fear of the Lord is upon the land." Exhaustion caught up with them. Salmon stretched out on his back, a soft blanket of grass beneath him. He could hardly keep his eyes open. "Our days in the wilderness are almost over." He filled his lungs with the rich, fragrant scent of the land. The sky was cerulean with wisps of white. *Oh, Lord, my God, You are bringing us home to a land You have prepared for us. You have laid out this gift before us. Give us the courage to take it.* Closing his eyes, Salmon drifted off to sleep while listening to the stream of living water.

And as he did so, he dreamed of a beautiful woman peering down at him from a window, her luxurious curly, black hair rippling in the wind.

Rahab saw Cabul and the king's men returning late the next afternoon, while the gates were still open. Even from a distance, they looked weary and defeated. She drew back so Cabul wouldn't see her as he passed below her window, heading for the gate.

"Rahab!"

She ignored him. She hoped he wouldn't come and question her or seek solace in her company. She wanted no further discourse with the fellow. The king had summoned her yesterday, and she had repeated her lie about the spies and her directions to his men. He believed her, and that had been the end of it.

Later that evening, Cabul knocked at her door. Hiding her fear, she opened the door long enough to find out if the king had thought the matter over further and become suspicious. When Cabul made it clear he had come for personal reasons, she told him she was ill and needed to be alone. It was no pretense. She was sick — sick of him, sick of the life she led, sick at the realization that everyone in this city would be dead soon because of their stubborn hearts and stiff-necked pride. She did not rejoice that destruction would come upon them, but she wanted to separate herself from them. She wanted to close herself in and stand at the window, waiting for her deliverance.

But there were others to consider, others to protect.

She let another night pass. On the third day, she ventured out of her house to shop in the marketplace, where she knew her father would be selling dried dates, raisins, and parched grains. When she approached him, he smiled briefly before returning his full attention to a patron standing at the booth. Her heart softened, for her father had never condemned her for the choices she made. Groveling for a living himself, he'd understood her reasons and never stopped loving her. Her mother had had grand hopes for her when the king had summoned her to his bed, but she'd put too much confidence in her daughter's physical beauty. Rahab had had no such illusions. Men were fickle, especially when they held positions of power, and she hadn't expected the affair to last long. She'd only hoped it would last long enough for her to make a place for herself in the king's service. It had, and now she had a livelihood and could help provide for her family — when their pride would allow it.

Neither her father nor her brothers had condemned her when she entered the king's chamber. Nor did they pity her when she left the king's house. They'd treated her with sad tolerance, until she showed she could manage independence and prosperity beyond their own. She'd been the one able to give money whenever it was needed, and she'd always made sure her mother, sisters, and sisters-in-law shared in the gifts she received from patrons. She'd never done so out of a feeling of compulsion or pride but out of love for them.

"How goes the day for you, my daughter?"

"It is a day of hope, Father."

"Hope is a good thing. Come and sit with an old man and tell me what news you've heard these past weeks." He set two stools out and sat on one, gesturing for her to take the other.

Rahab watched him rub his leg. The years of hard work showed on him, and he seemed to be in more pain today. But he would not thank her for mentioning it. "How is Mother?"

"In her glory, tending three grandchildren while your sisters beat and strip the flax."

"And my brothers?"

"At work on the ramparts."

No wonder he was rubbing his leg and pinched with pain. "You've been climbing the date palms again." What choice had he if the king summoned her brothers to work on the wall defenses and left an old man to carry the work of his sons?

"I've been training a grandson."

"Oh, Father. You're lucky you haven't broken your neck!"

"The king is in greater need than I."

"He can add all the fortifications in the world, and they won't help."

His hand stopped rubbing and his head came up. "The Israelites have settled in Shittim," he said.

"Not for much longer."

"No?"

"No. The Lord has given them this land."

His eyes flickered as he studied her face.

"I heard that spies entered the city several nights ago."

"By now, they will have given their report."

His eyes filled with fear. "Did you help them get away?"

She leaned forward and took his gnarled hands in hers. "I have seen the truth, Father. I know what's going to happen, the only thing that *can* happen. But I can't talk about it here. Come to my house before you leave the city. I have news that will give our family cause to celebrate."

His hands were cold as they tightened on hers. He searched her eyes. "What have you done, Daughter?"

"It's what will be done for us, provided we act in good faith. Come tonight and I'll tell you everything."

"They will come against Jericho?"

"Yes, Father, and they will destroy it." She stood and leaned down to kiss his cheek. "But our salvation is at hand."

Rahab's father brought her two brothers with him. She greeted them warmly and seated them on cushions set around a low table. She poured wine for them and encouraged them to eat.

"I'm not hungry," Mizraim said tersely. "Father said you summoned us."

"It wouldn't hurt to eat while we talk."

"Should we have an appetite when the Israelites are camped across the Jordan?"

Her youngest brother, Jobab, afraid and angry, looked up at her. "Father said you took in the spies. What possessed you to risk everything we've worked for? If the king finds out —"

"The king knows the spies were here at my house," she said, seeing three faces blanch. "He sent soldiers to take them, and I told his men they'd already left the city."

"Then they must have escaped," Mizraim said. "If they'd been captured, their bodies would be hanging on the wall by now."

Rahab smiled. "They weren't captured, because I hid them on my roof."

"You . . . what?" her father said weakly.

"I hid them, and then I let them down from my window and told them to hide in the hill country for three days before crossing the Jordan."

Her father and brothers stared at her. Mizraim came to his feet. "By the gods, what have you done to us?"

Jobab held his head in despair. "We'll all be destroyed for your treason."

"I've chosen the side that offers life," Rahab said.

"*Life?*" Mizraim said, his face red with

anger. "You don't know what you're talking about! What of *us?* Are we not able to choose?"

She restrained her anger. How many times had she come to the aid of her family, and Mizraim could still accuse her so? "That's why you're here." She set the jug of wine firmly in the middle of the table and sat with them. "Years ago, Father, you met an Israelite spy in the palm grove. You said you could see in his eyes that he would return."

"They did return and were defeated."

"Yes, but they came back without the Ark of their God. Isn't that what you told me?"

"Yes." Her father frowned, thinking back. "And Moses didn't lead them."

"I've heard Moses is dead," Mizraim said, taking a seat again.

"Do you think that matters?" Rahab was determined to make them understand that the arrangements she had made with the spies were their only chance for survival. "For all his greatness, Moses was only a man. It is the God of all creation who protects these people. The first time they came into the land, they entered like a band of thieves scattered across the ridges of the hill country. They were defeated because God was not with them. This time the

Israelites stand together. There's a new generation of Israelites out there across the river. They're waiting for their God to instruct them. Do not speak, Mizraim! Listen to what I'm telling you. When the time is right, the Israelites *will* cross the Jordan, and they *will* be victorious."

"They'll never take Jericho," Mizraim said, picking up his cup of wine. "I've been working on fortifications since the last full moon. You know yourself how tall and wide these walls are. No army can break through them!"

"You boast, but I see the fear in your eyes." She was not cowed by his angry glare. "What are these walls to a God who can part the seas? We've all heard the stories. God laid waste to Egypt with ten plagues. He spoke through Moses, and a nation was delivered from slavery. He opened the Red Sea so the Israelites crossed over on dry land. Have you ever heard of such power? Truly, He is God, the *only* God. You *must* know this! I've always told you everything I've heard. Think on what you know. Why else do you think our people quake in terror? You, among them."

"But this is *our* land!" Jobab said. "They have no right to it! We built these walls! We planted the crops and built the houses! Our father's father and his father before him harvested dates from the palm grove just beyond these walls!"

She wanted to shake them all. "We've bowed down to the baals all these years, thinking they were the owners of the land. But this land belongs to the God out there, and He's going to take it." She gave a bleak laugh. "Do you think we'll be safe because we've sacrificed to statues we carved and molded? What power have they over the elements?" She sneered. "They've never been anything more than mindless, heartless stone and clay idols." She slammed the palm of her hand on the table. "Well, now, the true landlord has revealed Himself. The God of the Israelites owns the land. He owns the palm trees and terebinths and grapevines; He owns the bees that make the honey; He owns the locusts that destroyed Egypt! Everything is His, and He can give the land and all that's on it to whomever He chooses. *And He has chosen those people across the river in Shittim!*"

They sat in stunned silence. Her father looked up at her. She could see he was trembling. "This is the news we came to hear, Daughter?"

"We should gather our families and have a feast together," Jobab said dismally. "We'll

82

lace the wine with hemlock and be spared the agony of being hacked to pieces by the swords of Israel."

"Bravely spoken," Mizraim said in disgust.

"We will live," Rahab said.

Mizraim picked up his cup of wine again. "How? The Israelites leave no survivors."

"I helped the spies escape, and they've promised to spare our lives when they take the city!"

"And you believed them?" Mizraim said. "Everyone knows they annihilate every living thing."

"They swore an oath to me."

"An oath is no better than the man who swears it!"

Rahab tipped her chin. "I know that better than you, my brother. I've had dealings with men since I was a girl."

"And brought shame upon us for it."

Her father slammed his fist on the table. "You'll listen to your sister! She is older than you and wiser in the world than all of us."

Mizraim winced and lowered his head.

"They were strangers," her father said. "Why should you trust them?"

"I asked the men to promise by the Lord, and they did so. Would any man dare swear a vain oath before this God? If they fail to keep their word, they'll answer to Him for it."

"Not that it'll matter much to us," Jobab said, still gloomy. "We'll be dead."

Rahab reached out and put her hand over her brother's. "You must decide where to place your faith, Jobab. You can have faith in the king of Jericho, who is but a man. Or you can put your faith in the King of Kings, the God of Israel. It's true, I don't know these men who came as spies, and I've only heard the stories about the Lord. But I believe what I've heard. Each time I heard of Him, I've experienced a quickening inside me, an assurance. I can't explain it any more than that, but I *know* this is God, the only God, and I've chosen to put my faith and hope in Him." She leaned back, looking at them. "You must decide for yourselves whether you choose life or death."

"We choose life," her father answered for them.

"We have one chance," Rahab said, "and that chance rests in the Lord God of Israel." Her heart beat strongly with excitement and thanksgiving. "We must make provisions for the days ahead. When the Israelites rescue us, we don't want to go to them empty-handed. Sell sparingly in the marketplace,

Father, and bring most of the grain, raisins, and dates here. I'll store them so that we have food when the siege begins and gifts for later." She nodded toward the far corner. "I've purchased a large storage jar for water, and I've gone to the spring each day in order to fill it. Have my sisters fill skins so there will be water enough for everyone."

She rose and went to the window, looking out toward the desert. "We'll make ourselves ready now. Have your possessions packed and ready to move. Stay girded and keep your weapon beside you at all times. When the Israelites cross the river, gather your wives and children and come here to my house." She turned. "Waste no time. We must separate ourselves from everyone in this city, for they are all marked for destruction. The two men from God promised me that everyone who's inside my house will live. Anyone outside it will perish."

Her father leaned forward, clasping his hands on the table. "There are a dozen windows in the wall, Rahab. How will the Israelites know this house from all the rest?"

Smiling, she lifted the crimson rope she'd tied in her window. "They will know us by this sign, and death will pass us by."

"There are twenty of us, Rahab. How're you going to make room for all of us and the provisions we'll need to survive?"

"Oh, Mizraim, you worry about so many things. You worry about what you're going to eat and where you're going to sleep. Only one thing is necessary. Obey the instructions we've been given! If you want to live, pack your belongings and come to my house." She smiled. "And in your haste, don't forget to bring Basemath and the children with you."

After three days, Salmon and Ephraim left the hill country and crossed the Jordan. Stripping off the Amorite garments, they donned their own clothing and ran the rest of the way to Shittim, where they found Joshua and Caleb together.

"The Lord will certainly give us the whole land," Ephraim said, panting heavily, "for all the people in the land are terrified of us!"

"Be at ease and rest." Joshua nodded for them to sit close to the fire. He was calm, his gaze steady, as though nothing they told him had changed anything.

Salmon's excitement was roaring within him so that he felt he could run through the entire camp, shouting the news to the thousands who waited to go into battle. "The land is ours, and it's rich beyond anything we've ever imagined! God has kept His promise. The hearts of the Canaanites have melted before the power of the Lord."

"A harlot in Jericho told us," Ephraim said, still breathing hard.

A harlot. Salmon didn't like the way Ephraim described Rahab.

Salmon had always thought it was Joshua's and Caleb's faith that had singled them out from all others among the chosen race, but a single evening in the company of a Jerichoan whore had made him realize that God could write His name upon the heart of anyone He chose — even a Canaanite prostitute! Out there in the darkness, across the Jordan inside the wall of a pagan city was a woman of contemptible reputation who'd never seen a miracle, tasted a bite of manna, or heard a single word of the Law. And yet her faith was strong enough that she had greeted, welcomed, and protected those who were coming to destroy her and her people. "The Lord your God is the supreme God of the heavens above and the earth below," she had declared.

"The woman's name is Rahab," Salmon said to the two venerable old warriors. "She called down to us from a window in the wall and met us just inside the gate, then took us into her house. She hid us on her roof before the soldiers came, then told them we'd left the city."

Ephraim quickly took up Rahab's defense as well. "The soldiers believed her lie and went chasing after shadows."

"She welcomed us with kindness and recommended we wait in the hill country for three days before returning to give you our report. It was this woman who said the Lord has given us the land. She said, 'The Lord your God is the supreme God of the heavens above and the earth below.' And she asked us to give an oath to save her family from death, an oath by the Lord."

Joshua's eyes narrowed slightly. "And did you give this oath?"

Salmon felt the sweat break out on the back of his neck. Had he overstepped himself and gone against the will of the Lord? "Yes, sir, we did give our oath." He swallowed hard. "If I have done wrong in this, I pray the Lord will hold me alone responsible and not punish this woman. We did swear before the Lord our God that anyone inside Rahab's house would be spared."

"Then it will be so," Joshua said.

Salmon breathed easier.

"How will we know her from the others?" Caleb asked.

Salmon turned to him eagerly. "We gave her a sign to use so that we'll know where her dwelling is. She used a scarlet cord to let us down to the ground, saving our lives and giving us a way of escape. I told Rahab to leave that same cord tied in her window. It will be easily seen from outside the walls."

Joshua rose. "The Lord protects those who belong to Him."

"Blessed be the name of the Lord," Salmon said, relieved.

Caleb tossed a branch onto the fire, sending up a burst of sparks. He stared into the flames, his hands clasped. Joshua glanced at his old kinsman and then came around the fire to Salmon. He put his hand on Salmon's shoulder. "You and Ephraim will both see to the safety of this woman and her family. The Lord spoke to me this morning, and I've given His instructions to the commanders of the tribes. You will hear them now. We cross the Jordan in three days. Make your preparations."

Ephraim watched Joshua walk away. "Our mission wasn't necessary. He had already decided what to do even before he heard our report."

Caleb snapped a branch in half. "Never question the ways of the Lord or the servants He has put over the people!" He glared at Ephraim and then at Salmon. "Joshua is God's instrument."

Salmon didn't share Ephraim's disappointment over lost glory for their deed. He'd been honored that Joshua had felt enough confidence in him to send him to Jericho at all. What did it matter that the Lord spoke to Joshua before they returned? Did God need their report? It seemed to Salmon that he and Ephraim had been sent to Jericho for another reason, a reason no one had known about except the Lord: God had sent them so they would find Rahab and open the way for her deliverance.

Caleb looked between them. "Which of you intends to take charge of the woman?"

"I will," Salmon said.

Caleb's eyes darkened.

"Blessings upon you, my brother," Ephraim said. "I'd be hard-pressed explaining to Havilah how I came to be in the company of a prostitute!" Laughing, he slapped Salmon on the back.

"I'm certain your brothers and sisters await your safe return," Caleb said.

Ephraim's amusement evaporated. "Yes, sir." He gave Salmon a quick, sympathetic glance as he strode off to rejoin his relatives.

Salmon waited for Caleb to speak his

mind. Since the death of Moses, there was no man other than Joshua whom Salmon respected more than this patriarch of his tribe, the tribe of Judah. Caleb was one of only two men to be found faithful among the slaves who had been delivered from Egypt.

The old man raised his head, his expression challenging. "She is a foreign woman. You know the warnings about foreign women."

"She wants to be one of us." Salmon wanted this man's confidence and approval. He debated within himself, and then decided the best course of action was to speak the truth about his feelings and seek Caleb's counsel. "I want to take this woman into my tent."

"One battle at a time, my son."

Salmon met his look. "I thought it best to discuss it now."

"She must be beautiful," Caleb said wryly. Salmon could feel the heat climbing into his face. The old man's smile turned cynical. "You blush like a boy."

Anger stirred Salmon to speak more boldly. "I'm twenty-six years old, and I've never met a woman who has so inclined me toward marriage."

Caleb shook his head, angry and aggrieved. "It's ever thus, Salmon. It's always the pagan women who draw our men away from God."

"Rahab isn't a pagan!"

"She is a Canaanite."

"This woman has acted with more faith than my father or mother. But let's lay out all the objections at once. She's older than I, and she's made her living as a prostitute!"

Caleb's eyes shone strangely. "And you would choose such a woman to be your wife?"

"Rahab is a woman of excellence."

"Excellence?"

"She proclaimed her faith by her actions."

Caleb poked the fire with a stick. "Perhaps she's merely a cunning liar who's betrayed her people in order to save her own skin."

"Who are her people?"

When Caleb raised his hand as though to wave Salmon's words away, Salmon plunged ahead in his defense of Rahab. "It is God's will we are to follow. You and Joshua are the ones who have taught me that. And that's what I seek to do: God's will. Help me find it where this woman is concerned!"

Caleb let out his breath slowly and rubbed his face. "Joshua has already given the command. You will see to the woman's safety and that of those who are with her. And if you choose, she will belong to you by right of conquest."

Salmon's heart beat strongly. He felt he'd been handed a precious gift, despite the coolness of Caleb's proclamation.

Caleb lowered his hands and looked at him gravely. "You will leave this woman and her relatives outside the camp. Perhaps she will go her own way and take her family with her."

"She will want to become one of us."

"How can you be so certain?"

Salmon hunkered down. "I saw her eyes. I heard her voice." He wanted Caleb to trust Rahab as he did. "Were we not slaves when God delivered us? I believe God sent Ephraim and me into Jericho to find this woman. It's the only reason that makes sense to me, considering that God spoke to Joshua before we returned to give our report. The Lord wants this woman delivered from the evil of the Canaanites, just as He delivered us from Egypt."

"Be careful not to add to what the Lord has said, Salmon. You must align yourself with the will of God — not the desires of your own heart. My generation thought they could have their own way, and they all died in the desert."

"The will of God is ever in my mind. From the time I was a small boy, you've taught me the truth and lived it before my eyes. One thing has always been clear to me. It was not because we had merit or deserved freedom that the Lord delivered us from Egypt. The Lord saved us out of *His* great mercy." Salmon held his hands out. "Would the Lord not extend His mercy to anyone who yearns to belong to Him? I saw this yearning in Rahab. I heard it in her voice. She *believes* the Lord is God, and she declared her allegiance to Him by saving us, His servants." He paused, weighing his next words carefully. Finally he spoke the question that had been burning on his heart for the past three days. "Could it not be that God has aligned the desire of my heart with His good purpose toward this woman?"

Caleb considered his words. "You're only guessing about the desires of this woman's heart, Salmon."

"It is a sign of wisdom that she is in awe of the Lord. Could Rahab truly declare that the Lord is the only God — the God of the heavens above and the earth below — if God Himself had not written His name upon her heart?"

"If you seek a quick answer from me, my

son, I have none. We must both pray and seek God's will in this matter."

Salmon struggled against the urgency he felt. "If anyone finds out she's given aid to Ephraim and me, she may not survive long enough to be rescued. I should go back —"

"Did she ask this of you?"

"No, but —"

Caleb's eyes blazed. "Then I would ask you this: where is *your* faith, Salmon? If it is indeed God's plan to deliver this woman, *He will do it.*"

Salmon started to say more but was silenced when he looked into Caleb's eyes. He had said enough already. The lines in the old man's face showed wisdom earned by years of suffering. The sins of others, including those of Salmon's own father and mother, had caused Caleb and Joshua greater heartache than he would ever know. It had been almost forty years since Joshua and Caleb had received the promise that they would be the only ones of their generation to set foot in the Promised Land. Two out of an entire people. All because the others had refused to believe the promise God had given them.

"I believe the Lord will protect her," Salmon said, lowering his head. "May God forgive my unbelief."

"I was young and impetuous once," Caleb said more gently. "You must learn to be patient. God doesn't need our help."

Salmon raised his head and smiled. "When you meet Rahab, you'll understand what I see in her."

"*If* I meet Rahab, I'll know it is by God's will — not by your efforts — that her life has been spared." He stood. "It's late, and we both need to rest. There is much to do tomorrow. We must make our preparations for the days ahead."

Salmon rose with him, but didn't move away from the fire. He wanted Caleb's blessing for his plans regarding Rahab. "Then you have no objections to my taking Rahab into my tent?"

Caleb gave him a rueful stare. "It would be wise to wait and see what choice *she* makes."

"She's already made her choice."

"Indeed, and if God delivers Rahab from Jericho, it will be left to her to decide what to do with the life God grants her." His mouth tipped up in a gentle smile. "If she is as wise as you say, she will prefer an older man."

Salmon laughed, all the tension falling away. Had Caleb merely been testing him?

"You said she belonged to me by right of conquest."

Caleb laughed with him. "Ah, that's true, but a woman with her faith and courage will have a mind of her own." He clamped his hand upon Salmon's shoulder, his expression serious again. "When the battle is over, Joshua will decide her fate. Her true motives will be put to the test." He let go of him. "If she is as you say she is, then you needn't concern yourself over the outcome."

Salmon felt less than satisfied. He'd wanted a firm answer, and instead he had been told to wait.

Would Rahab prove to be the woman he thought she was? If not, it would no doubt fall to him to make sure she didn't trouble Israel again.

Four

Rahab poured grain into the pottery bin Mizraim's son had brought her. Two more baskets, and the jar would be full. Three large storage jars contained water. She had two baskets full of dates and two more of raisins. Over the past few days her mother, her sisters, and her brothers' wives had brought beans, lentils, onions, garlic, and leeks. Her house was beginning to look like one of the booths in the marketplace, loaded with foodstuffs for sale. But would there be enough if the siege lasted longer than a week? She looked around again, taking mental inventory of what she had and what more she might still need to take care of her family until the Israelites could break through the gates and come to their rescue. Time was short, and each day that passed increased her feelings of urgency — and excitement.

Jobab and Mizraim came to her each

evening after their labor on the walls. As she served them a meal, they told her what they'd heard. Every bit of information she could glean might become important later. Most important was to encourage her father and brothers to trust in the God of Israel and not to put their confidence in the king's plans.

"The king's convinced we're all safe," Mizraim said one evening. "The Israelites have never faced a wall so high and thick as this one."

Jobab tore off a piece of bread and dipped it in the lentil stew Rahab had prepared. "They may not even be able to reach the walls. The king has thousands of arrows made and ready for the attack. The entire army will be standing on the battlements, ready to shoot any man who dares come close."

"Don't fool yourself, brother." Rahab replenished his wine. "Don't put your trust in that man to save us. I know him better than you, remember? Besides, he and all his soldiers and weapons won't mean a thing when the Israelites come against us. They have God on their side. Do as I've told you. Drop everything and come here when the Israelites step foot on the west bank of the Jordan."

"But how are they going to get to the west bank?"

"I don't know!" Rahab set the jug down and put her hands on her hips. "Maybe they'll build rafts. Maybe they'll swim across. Maybe they'll *walk* across!"

Mizraim laughed. "Maybe eagles will come and carry them across. Or better yet, maybe they'll sprout wings and fly!"

"You dare laugh?" Rahab smacked him on the back of his head. "If God can part the Red Sea, do you think that river will stop Him? He could dry it up with one breath! The only safe place outside the camp of Israel is right here where you're sitting." She took the jug and glared at her two brothers in frustration. Why wasn't it as clear to them as it was to her? "God is coming! And you'd better be ready when He gets here!"

Jobab pushed his stool back and stood. He looked around the room at the storage jars, the rush mats stacked in the corner, the blankets piled on her bed. "What more do we need?"

She closed her eyes tightly, trying to still the trembling inside her. "Patience." If the Israelites crossed the Jordan at this very moment, it would not be too soon for her.

■ ■ ■ ■

While the Israelites remained camped in Shittim, manna continued to rain down from heaven, though it lessened each day until only a soft sprinkling appeared like dew as the sun rose.

Salmon went down onto his knees with the thousands of other men, women, and children who gathered their share for the day. He made a cake of the coriander-like flakes of manna and placed it on the camp stove his parents had brought out of Egypt. He thought of his parents often now, praying he wouldn't make the same mistakes, praying he would stand in faith, praying he would not weaken in the face of battling the enemy, praying he would be a man of God, not just a man.

Breathing in the wonderful, sweet aroma as the manna cake sizzled in olive oil, he took a pronged stick and carefully turned the cake. His stomach clenched with hunger. When the cake was finished, he rolled it up and sat back to eat it slowly, savoring its sweetness. Soon the manna would disappear altogether, for the people would have no need of it when they entered Canaan, a land of milk and honey. Milk meant herds of cattle and goats; honey meant blooming fruit trees, vines, and crops of grain and vegetables, foods his generation had heard of but had never tasted. The Lord had said they would take possession of orchards and vineyards they hadn't planted, harvest the wheat and beans and lentils another nation had sown, shepherd herds and flocks left by the fleeing enemies of God. Yet Salmon couldn't help but feel a deepening sadness.

He'd never known anything but the taste of manna. The first time he had tasted anything else was the day he and Ephraim had camped alongside the stream in Canaan, where they'd caught and roasted fish. Though the meal had been delicious, it couldn't compare with what God had given them and what God would soon take away.

Salmon held the bread of heaven reverently. All his life he had taken it for granted; now he realized how precious it was. As he ate of it, tears came, for he knew this bread had come from the very hand of God, a free gift keeping him alive. Could there ever be anything as sweet? Could anything else be as nourishing?

Soon the people would cease to be children wandering in the desert and stand as men and women of God in the land of promise. And like mother's milk, the manna would be taken from them. He and the others would plow, plant, tend herds and flocks, and harvest crops. They would have children, build homes, build cities.

Oh, God, keep us faithful! he prayed. *Don't let us again become whining infants! Don't let us become arrogant in the victories You will give us. The sins of our fathers are ever before us. If only they could be wiped away once and for all time, so that we could stand in Your presence the way Adam and Eve did, when first You created them.*

And the shofar blew, calling the people to gather.

The time had come to move forward and receive the gift God had so graciously prepared for them.

Officers came through the camp, calling down the orders from Joshua. "When you see the Levitical priests carrying the Ark of the Covenant of the Lord your God, follow them. Since you have never traveled this way before, they will guide you. Stay about a half mile behind them, keeping a clear distance between you and the Ark. Make sure you don't come any closer."

Salmon quickly took down his tent, rolled the leather around the poles, and secured it to his pack. He shouldered his load and stood waiting with thousands of others from the tribe of Judah. He felt a rush of strength and longed to run to the river, but he held his place, keeping the heat banked within him.

The Ark of the Covenant passed before them, and he felt tingling excitement in his soul. The priests carried the Ark toward the Jordan River. At the prescribed distance, the tribes began to follow. The land was alive with the moving populace, thousands walking with an assurance of victory.

They camped near the Jordan, and Joshua spoke to the people. "Purify yourselves, for tomorrow the Lord will do great wonders among you."

Men separated from their wives and washed their garments. Salmon was among the multitude of men. He fasted from everything but the small portion of manna he had gathered that morning and spent the evening inside his tent, alone and in prayer.

When the sun rose, Salmon stood once again among the thousands, waiting to hear Joshua proclaim the Word of the Lord. *"Sons of Israel, come and hear the words of the Lord your God!"*

Salmon moved forward with his brothers and cousins so they were shoulder to shoulder. Joshua raised his hands, his voice strong and carrying to the farthest members of the congregation. "Come and listen to what the Lord your God says. Today you will know that the living God is among you. He will surely drive out the Canaanites, Hittites, Hivites, Perizzites, Girgashites, Amorites, and Jebusites. Think of it! The Ark of the Covenant, which belongs to the Lord of the whole earth, will lead you across the Jordan River! The priests will be carrying the Ark of the Lord, the Lord of all the earth. When their feet touch the water, the flow of water will be cut off upstream, and the river will pile up there in one heap."

At Joshua's command, the priests carrying the Ark started out once again toward the river.

Salmon stretched his neck to watch. His heart pounded. He feared God as much as he loved Him. Whenever the Ark was carried before Salmon, he trembled with an inexplicable excitement. His skin tingled. The hair on the back of his neck rose. He'd grown up seeing the cloud lift from the tabernacle, giving the sign that the people were to move their camp. He'd seen the pillar of fire at night. But he hadn't been born yet when his people left Egypt. He hadn't seen the miracles done there or the parting of the Red Sea so that the Israelites could cross on dry land. He trembled, his breathing shaky, anticipating how the Lord would enable His people to cross the rushing torrent of the Jordan.

The Ark was far ahead of the people. Was God showing them that He didn't need their protection? Had the people been allowed, they would have clustered tightly around the Ark as it moved, but it was out there ahead, the gold shimmering in the sunlight and showing them the way. As they came closer to the river, everyone grew quieter. No one moved, no one spoke as they watched and waited for the command to go forward.

The priests reached the bank of the Jordan. They didn't hesitate but walked straight into the flooded Jordan. And as they did, there was a roaring sound such as Salmon had never heard in all his life. The hair stood on the back of his neck as he saw the water draw back, a hiss of steam billowing up. Walking in faith, the priests carried the Ark of the Covenant of the Lord to the center of the riverbed and stopped there, planting their feet. The golden Ark glistened in the morning sunlight.

And thousands upon thousands followed.

When the people were safely across the river, Joshua announced that the Lord had told him to choose twelve men, one from each tribe. As head of the tribe of Judah, Caleb called out the name of the man who would represent them. Jedidiah pressed forward. He was easily seen, taller and stronger than all the rest, and the men of Judah slapped him on the back and gave him room to walk to the front of the tribe and stand beside Caleb. The old man put his hand on Jedidiah's shoulders, spoke to him softly, and released him. Jedidiah ran ahead and joined the eleven other tribal representatives near Joshua.

"Go into the middle of the Jordan, in front of the Ark of the Lord your God," Joshua called out to the twelve representatives of the tribes. "Each of you must pick up one stone and carry it out on your shoulder — twelve stones in all, one for each of the twelve tribes. We will use these stones to build a memorial. In the future, your children will ask, 'What do these stones mean to you?' Then you can tell them, 'They remind us that the Jordan River stopped flowing when the Ark of the Lord's covenant went across.' These stones will stand as a permanent memorial among the people of Israel."

Joshua and the twelve men strode forward.

■ ■ ■ ■

Rahab heard someone screaming and ran to the window. Leaning out, she saw a soldier running up the road. *"They're coming! They're coming! The Israelites are heading for the river!"* On the east side of the Jordan, a cloud of dust rose as a mass of people headed for the river, but what caught her attention was something ahead of them, something that shone brightly and sent shafts of light in all directions! Was it the Ark of the Lord that she had heard about?

Her lips parted as she saw two lines of steam shoot into the air and move back from the small figures now moving down into the riverbed. Her skin tingled as a rush of emotions took hold of her. Fear. Exaltation. Awe. She was laughing and crying at the same time. Her heart galloped. She leaned so far out the window, she almost toppled. *A miracle.* She was seeing a miracle! "What a mighty God He is!" she cried out as men shouted from the ramparts.

Steam continued to rise, forming a cloud over the river. Panic-stricken, people outside the walls were screaming and running toward the city like a stampeding flock. Did she hear, or only imagine, the sound of a ram's horn? The army of Israelites was crossing the Jordan. There were thousands upon thousands of them spreading out across the plains of Moab. They were as many as the stars in the heavens. They moved quickly but in order.

Rahab looked away and craned her neck toward the grove of palms. "Come, Father, come on. Where are you?" Farmers and workers were running toward Jericho. She slapped her hands on the windows, fighting against her impatience. Finally she saw him. Her mother followed, and both were struggling beneath burdens of belongings.

"Leave everything!" Rahab shouted. *"Come as you are!"*

It was useless to yell. They couldn't hear her above the din of panicked citizens descending upon the already overcrowded gates. She waved frantically. Her father saw her but dropped nothing. Tiring, her mother slid her heavy bundle to the ground and began dragging it behind her.

"Run!" Rahab gestured wildly. "Everything you need is here!"

They plodded along, stubbornly hanging on to everything they owned. Rahab cursed in frustration. A crowd was pressing through the gates. Someone was shrieking. Someone had probably fallen and was now being trampled. They sounded like a mob of wild animals, fists flying as those who were stronger tried to beat their way ahead of everyone else.

Someone banged on her door. "Rahab!" Mizraim called. "Let us in!"

She yanked the bar up and opened the door so that he and his wife, Basemath, could enter. They were carrying their two children. Jobab and his wife, Gowlan, were hurrying down the street, shouting for their children to hurry ahead. They all looked wild-eyed and pale with fear, and everyone carried something. Rahab shook her head at their choices as they entered her house: a pot; a painted urn; a basket containing a kohl bottle, tweezers, an ointment box, jewelry, and a horn of oil.

Mizraim's baby boy screamed until Basemath sat on Rahab's bed and nursed him. When footsteps raced across Rahab's roof, Mizraim's daughter dropped the urn. It shattered on the floor. Mizraim shouted at her. Crying hysterically, the little girl ran to her mother and clung to her.

"Hush, Mizraim. You're behaving as badly as those madmen at the gate. You're only frightening the children more." Rahab scooped up the little girl and hugged her. "We're all safe here, Bosem." She kissed her cheek. "Everything will be all right." She waved her hand, beckoning the others. "Come on, children. All of you. I have some things for you." She set Bosem on her feet and put out a basket of painted sticks and knucklebones. "Awbeeb, my sweet, come play with your cousins."

Rahab's sisters, Hagri and Gerah, and their husbands, Vaheb and Zebach, arrived with their children in tow. "People are going mad out there!" Seeing the others, the boys and girls joined their cousins in their games of knucklebones and pickup sticks.

"Where are Father and Mother?" Jobab said.

"I lost sight of them when they joined the crowd at the gate," Rahab answered, nodding toward the window as she took the baby from Basemath. "See if you can spot them, Mizraim." She lifted the child to her shoulder and held him close, patting his back and pacing.

"I heard the guards are going to close the gate," Jobab said.

"They'll let everyone in," Rahab said calmly. "The king will want every able-bodied worker inside before the gates are closed. If his army perishes, he'll have the citizenry standing on the walls and throwing rocks." She was angry that her father hadn't done as she told him. He and her mother should have dropped everything and come running with the first cry of that soldier running up the road. Had they listened, they would have been spared the violence at the gate. She hoped they wouldn't be hurt in the pushing and shoving mob trying to get inside the city walls.

"I'll go out and find them," Mizraim said. "Bar the door behind me, Zebach."

When an hour passed and he hadn't returned, Basemath began weeping.

"As soon as Father and Mother make it into the city, he'll come back," Rahab said, trying to stay calm for the children's sake. She could see the throng from her window and knew the city was filling with those who lived outside the walls. Even traveling merchants and caravans were clamoring to be let in.

"Let us in!" It was Mizraim. The women all sighed in relief as Zebach threw the bar off and yanked it open. Basemath ran to her disheveled husband and sobbed against his torn tunic. Rahab's father was just behind him, his face bleeding.

Rahab poured some water into a bowl and then saw her mother dragging her bundle into the house. Thrusting the bowl into Hagri's hands, Rahab strode across the room. "What's so important you'd risk your lives to bring it with you?" she demanded, reaching for the bundle.

"No!" Her mother slapped her hands away, crying out. "No, no!"

Rahab fought tears of exasperation. She was so relieved to see them safe and yet so angry at their foolishness. She forced herself to display a calm she was far from feeling. "Here. Let me take it. I'll be careful. Let go!"

Weeping, her mother sank to the floor, exhausted. She covered her head with her shawl and sobbed.

Her father brushed away Hagri's attempts to aid him and stumbled wearily to the window. "Did you see it? Did you see what happened? The water rolled back like a carpet, toward the town of Adam and the Salt Sea."

"I saw," Rahab said. "The hand of God has come upon the land, and He will brush away His enemies like stones on a game table."

Her father turned away from the window and sat heavily on the step she'd built. Rahab had never seen him so exhausted. He was trembling, and his face was sweating profusely. "You're right, Rahab. They will destroy us. They're coming across the plains of Moab like locusts, and they'll destroy everything in their path."

"Hush, Father." Everyone was frightened enough without his fanning the flames of doom. She took the bowl of water from Hagri and knelt down before her father. She spoke loudly enough for all to hear. "As long as we stay inside this house, we're safe." Squeezing out the cloth, she dabbed his face gently.

"Never have I seen such a thing in all my life." Still shaking, he closed his eyes and swallowed. "Never have I even dreamed of seeing such a thing as happened today." He made fists on his knees, his body rigid with fear. "Never have I beheld such a terrifying God as this!"

"And the men who serve this God have promised to spare us." Setting the bowl aside, Rahab put her hands over his, gripping them tightly. "Remember the crimson cord that hangs out of my window. When the day of destruction comes, we will not perish."

The multitude stood on the west bank in Gilgal, east of Jericho, and watched as each of the twelve tribal representatives shouldered the largest stone he could carry and brought it into the midst of the camp. There the stones were set upright in a line, side by side, as a memorial of what God had done that day. Joshua took twelve men back down into the dry riverbed, where they piled up twelve more stones to remember the place where the Lord had brought them across the Jordan.

When the priests carried the Ark of the Covenant forward out of the dry riverbed, the sound of many waters came rushing. The river rumbled, racing down the riverbed from north and south, smashing together over the twelve stones. Once again, the Jordan overflowed its banks.

Joining thousands of others, Salmon cried out with joy as the Ark of the Covenant of the Lord came into the camp called Gilgal. The multitude raised their hands and voices in worship to the Lord God of Abraham, Isaac, and Jacob, the God who had brought them into the Promised Land.

Inside the walls of Jericho, the people waited, paralyzed with fear. Those who hadn't been able to get inside the city before the gates were shut and the beams rammed into place had fled over the mountain road to find protection among the kingdoms in the hill country. Some would go as far as the Mediterranean. And everywhere they traveled, they spread the news: The God of Israel dried up the Jordan River so the Hebrews could cross over!

The Israelites are in Canaan!

FIVE

Caleb gathered all the men and boys of Judah. "We have entered Canaan on the day of preparations for Passover, and Joshua has received these instructions from the Lord: the entire male population of Israel must be circumcised."

All those present knew that their fathers, who had been circumcised upon leaving Egypt, had lived under God's wrath because they continued to think and act like slaves rather than as free men chosen to be a holy nation. Thus, the fallen generation had not been allowed to circumcise their sons. But now the promise was about to be fulfilled. The hand of God would bring the seed of Israel safely into the land of Canaan. But before that could happen, God wanted His people to become a circumcised nation once again.

Salmon stood waiting among thousands of his brethren. There were males of all ages, from babes in arms to men ten years older than his twenty-six years. To keep himself from thinking about the knife, he looked at the walls of Jericho. Would it matter if the enemy knew he and all the rest of the warriors would be incapacitated for a few days? They would be vulnerable and easily defeated, just as the Shechemites had been four centuries ago when Jacob's sons took vengeance over the rape of their sister. Yet Salmon felt no fear. God had performed a miracle before Jerichoan eyes. They wouldn't dare open the gates and come out against Him. No, they would stay tightly holed up in their walled city. They were paralyzed with fear. The enemy would watch as Israel was circumcised. Let them watch, tremble, and do nothing. Passover was coming, and all Israel would remember the night the angel of death had passed over the Hebrew slaves who'd painted their door lintels with the lamb's blood, moving on to strike down all the firstborn of Egypt.

A boy cried out in pain. Salmon winced in sympathy. Six men went ahead of him before it was his turn.

"Salmon," Caleb said solemnly as he approached. After performing the rite, Caleb blessed him. "Just as you have entered into the covenant, so may you enter into marriage and good deeds."

"May the Lord make me His servant!" Salmon steadied himself before standing. For one second, he was sure he would faint and humiliate himself, but the light-headed sensation passed quickly. He returned to his tent and knelt on his mat. Bowing his head to the ground, he thanked God that he was one of His chosen people.

By the end of the day, he lay upon his mat, every movement causing pain. Every male had been circumcised. The Israelites were now freeborn children of God, no longer tainted by the idolatry of Egypt.

The covenant had been renewed.

"Give me that!" Rahab yanked a clay idol from her sister's hand and marched to the window.

"What are you doing?" Hagri cried out, getting up and racing after Rahab. "No!"

"What do you mean by bringing this wretched thing into my house?" Rahab hurled the false god out the window and watched it explode into pieces on the rocky ground below.

Hagri blanched. "The gods will avenge your disrespect!"

"If that thing held any power, would it have let me toss it out the window? Use the head you were born with, Hagri. Do you think that idol can bring us harm? It's nothing but clay. There is only one God, and He is the God of heaven and earth. He's the God who rolled back the Jordan a few days ago! Have you forgotten so quickly? Bow down to *Him!*"

Her father and mother and sisters and brothers and their children were all staring at her in frightened confusion. She was so angry she was shaking, but shouting at them wasn't going to make them understand. Why were they so stiff-necked and foolish? Why were they so stubborn?

She strove to speak calmly. "Our only hope is in the God of the Hebrews. We must get rid of everything that insults Him. Have you any other idols hidden among your possessions?" When they just stared at her and said nothing, she almost erupted in fury. "Spread out your things! Let me see what abominations you've brought into my house!"

Grudgingly, they began spreading out their possessions a few at a time. Vaheb, Hagri's husband, set out a clay-filled skull with shell eyes. "My father," he said when Rahab looked at it. "He was a wise man."

"Wise and *dead.*"

"Our ancestors advise us!"

"To do what? Become like them? Do you think that skull filled with dirt can tell you the way to escape the coming judgment? *Get rid of it!*"

"It's my father!"

"Your father is dead, Vaheb. A pity his head wasn't buried with him."

"Rahab!" her father said. "You've said enough!"

"I will have said and done enough when these things are thrown out that window!" Her brothers and sisters protested, but she outshouted them. "Should I have your deaths upon my conscience? Listen to me! All of you! That skull filled with *dirt* is nothing but a filthy idol and an insult to the God of the Hebrews. Get rid of it! *Get it out of my house!*"

"Abiasaph!" Vaheb appealed to Rahab's father. "Do you agree with her?"

Rahab felt the heat rush into her face as they turned away from her leadership. She pointed to the window. "Look out there! How many thousands do you see? And they all *walked* across the Jordan River, which is now flooded again. Do you wish to trust the God who brought them to the plains of Jericho, or do you want to trust a dead man's skull?"

No one said anything for a moment. Then

her father spoke. "Do as Rahab says."

Vaheb pleaded, "What if I hide it among my things and keep it out of sight? Then it won't offend you."

"You and that idol you cling to can get out of my house."

"You'd put us out?" He looked up, stricken and angry. "Your own sister and our children? You are a hard woman!"

Her eyes burned with tears. "They can follow you and your dead ancestors out that door, or they can trust almighty God to save them and stay here with me." She looked around at the others. "And that goes for the rest of you, too. You must decide. Our people sacrifice day and night in the hope that their gods can protect them if the walls cannot. Clay idols cannot fight a living God."

She pointed at the skull in Vaheb's hands. "Look into those shell eyes, my brother. Can they look back at you? Has that jaw ever opened and spoken words of wisdom? Can that skull *think?* It's a dead thing! Three days ago, we saw a true miracle. Put your hope in the God who brought the Israelites across the Jordan, the God who dwells in their camp. That God is going to give them Jericho."

"I'm afraid!" Gerah wept against her

husband, Zebach.

"We're all afraid," Rahab said more gently. "But fear the Lord who has the power to destroy us rather than these *things.* We've clung to useless, lifeless idols for too long. Do you think the God of heaven and earth will show mercy if we dishonor Him by having these things in our midst? We've separated ourselves from everyone in the city, and now we must remove all the unclean things from among us. Get rid of your false gods, Mama. Look to the God of Israel for salvation, Vaheb!"

Rahab's father rose slowly and came to her mother. "We must do likewise, Dardah. Give the idols to me."

"But, Abiasaph . . ."

"They almost cost us our lives getting into the city. Rahab is right." When he held his hands out, she opened the bundle she had dragged into the city, displaying an idol case and six round objects carefully wrapped in sheepskin. Rahab shuddered. As a child, she'd been afraid of the skulls of her ancestors with their dead eyes. They'd always held a place of prominence in her father's house, gruesome reminders of the past generations.

"Surely we could keep the box," her mother said.

"Why?" Rahab said.

"It's costly and beautiful. This is ivory and these stones are —"

Rahab wasn't willing to compromise. "It will only serve as a reminder of the unclean thing it held."

Her father dropped it out the window. The box cracked open and the stone statue bounced out and rolled down the slope. Next, her father dropped the skulls. One by one, they were smashed on the rocky ground below.

Rahab looked around again. "Remove the talismans from the children, Gerah."

Gerah did so and handed them to her to toss out the window. Rahab's spirit lifted and warmth filled her. Her relatives searched the room for anything that might be offensive to the God of the Hebrews. She turned away, overcome with emotion. If only she could throw away all the experiences of her life, leaving them behind like those broken idols on the hard ground outside the window. Her life was fraught with idols — her quest for money and security, her ability to mentally stand outside herself as she allowed her body to be used by countless men, her willingness to serve a king who saw his people as possessions meant to serve him. Oh, if only she could start afresh, be a new creation before this living God. If only she could be cleansed of all unrighteousness so that she could bow down before Him in thanksgiving instead of shame.

Blinking back tears, Rahab gazed out the window again. She stretched out her hands toward the tent in which the golden box had been placed. *O God of Israel, how I long to kneel before You. Whatever offering You require of me, I will give it, even my life. I have opened the gates of my heart and soul, for only You are worthy of praise, only You.*

Mizraim caught her around the waist and drew her back inside. "The guards might see —"

"Let them see." Shoving his hands away, Rahab stepped up again and stretched out her hands. Let *Him* see.

After the solemn rite of circumcision, the children of Israel celebrated the Passover — a feast marking the anniversary of their exodus from Egypt.

Salmon girded his loins, donned his sandals, and joined his older brothers, their wives and young children. His unmarried sister, Leah, would complete their family circle. Amminadab, the eldest, killed the Passover lamb at twilight. His wife prepared the bitter herbs and unleavened bread. As the lamb roasted over the fire, the family gathered close for the traditional retelling of the events leading up to the deliverance from slavery.

"Why is this night different from all others?" the youngest boy said, leaning against his father, Salmon's second brother.

"Forty years ago, our fathers and mothers were instructed by God to paint the blood of a lamb on their door lintels." Amminadab spoke carefully so the children would understand. "That way, when the angel of death came to strike down all the firstborn of Egypt, he would pass over the people of Israel."

Another child settled into the lap of her mother. "Were we always slaves?"

"Our father, Jacob, was a wandering Aramean long before our people went to Egypt. Jacob had two wives and two concubines, who bore him twelve sons, the patriarchs of the tribes who are gathered here now. Ten of these sons, including our father, Judah, were jealous of their younger brother, Joseph, so they sold him to a band of Ishmaelites traveling to Egypt. Joseph became the slave of Potiphar, captain of the palace guard, but the Lord blessed him in all he did. Even when Potiphar's wife falsely accused Joseph of a terrible crime and Potiphar sentenced him to prison, God continued to bless Joseph. And during the time of his slavery and imprisonment, God was preparing Joseph to deliver his father and brothers from death."

The children came and sat closer around Amminadab, drawn into the story of their history.

"After a time, Pharaoh was plagued by bad dreams. One of his servants told him Joseph could explain them, so Pharaoh had Joseph brought to him. The Lord revealed to Joseph the meaning of the dreams: a great famine would come upon Egypt and all the surrounding nations. The Lord also told Joseph how to save Egypt from starvation. When Pharaoh saw that Joseph was the wisest man in all the land, he made him overseer of all Egypt."

Amminadab's wife turned the spitted lamb slowly as he continued.

"It was during the famine that the sons of Jacob came to Egypt to buy grain. Joseph forgave their sins against him and told them to come to Egypt to live. Pharaoh gave them the land of Goshen, the most fertile land in all Egypt."

He sat the youngest boy on his knee. "In time, Joseph and his brothers died, but their descendants had many children and grand-children until Israel became a strong nation. A new pharaoh arose who didn't remember how Joseph had saved Egypt. This pharaoh saw our people as a threat and made them slaves. He put brutal slave drivers over us because he wanted to destroy our people by heavy work. But the Lord blessed us even in our oppression, and we thrived. The Egyptians became afraid and made our slavery even more bitter. They forced us to make bricks and mortar and work long hours in the fields. Even this didn't satisfy Pharaoh. So he gave the Hebrew midwives orders to kill all the baby boys as soon as they were born. But these women feared God more than Pharaoh, and they refused to do it. Then Pharaoh gave orders that all the young Israelite boys be killed."

Amminadab put his hand on one of the boys close to him. "Thousands of children were thrown into the Nile River. Little babies like your brother Samuel. But there was a brave woman named Jochebed who hid her son for three months. When she couldn't hide him any longer, she covered a wicker basket with tar and pitch, and placed him in it. Then she set it afloat among the reeds. And that's where the daughter of

Pharaoh found him."

"Moses!" the children all said at once, laughing and clapping their hands.

"Yes, the child was Moses," Amminadab said quietly. His solemnity made the children go quiet again. "Moses was the chosen servant of the Lord, the one who brought Israel the Law God wrote upon the stone tablets with His own finger on Mount Sinai, the Law for which the Ark of the Covenant was made." He ran his hand gently over the hair of his daughter and looked at the other boys and girls. "It is because our fathers and mothers broke faith with God that we've wandered almost forty years in the wilderness. It is because they refused to believe and obey that they all died in the wilderness. The Law is written so that we can study it and know how to live to please God."

"The Law is meant to be written upon our hearts as well," Salmon said.

His brother glanced up at him. "If such a thing is possible."

Salmon thought of Rahab. She didn't know the Law, and yet she was exhibiting the heart of it. *Love the Lord your God with all your heart, all your mind, and all your strength.* How could Rahab have such faith unless God Himself had given it to her as a gift? Could anyone grasp the ways of God with human understanding? Could anyone account for His great mercy? Rahab was a pagan, marked for death, and yet the Lord was seeing to it that death would pass over her.

"The Lord sent Moses to Pharaoh. Moses told Pharaoh to let our people go," Amminadab went on, "but Pharaoh wouldn't listen."

Another brother, Nahshon, stepped forward with a glass of wine. He hunkered down and began to pour the wine slowly onto the ground. "The Lord God poured out his wrath upon Egypt in ten plagues: water became blood; frogs and lice came; beasts of the field died; disease, boils, hail, locusts descended; darkness came when it should have been day; and finally came the slaying of all the firstborn of Egypt." The last of the wine stained the ground.

"Before each plague," Amminadab said, "the Lord gave Pharaoh another opportunity to repent and let our people go, but each time his heart grew harder and more arrogant, more defiant. When the last plague was coming upon Egypt, the Lord instructed us through Moses to kill a perfect lamb and paint our door lintels with its blood. That night when the angel of death came, he saw the blood and passed over all Israel."

"Why do you cry, Mama?"

"I cry over the suffering of our fathers and mothers under slavery, but I cry, too, for all those who died because Pharaoh held power over them."

"All Egypt was laid waste because Pharaoh's heart was hard," Amminadab said. "He had no mercy upon Israel, nor did he have mercy upon his own people."

"Some of them came with us," Nahshon said.

Amminadab's eyes flashed. "And most died in the desert because they couldn't give up worshiping their idols." He looked at Salmon. "They led our people astray!"

Heat poured into Salmon's face. Everyone had heard about Rahab. "Our own nature leads us astray," he said gently. "The Lord says, 'Hear, O Israel! The Lord is our God, the Lord alone. And you must love the Lord your God with all your heart, all your soul, and all your strength. And you must commit yourselves wholeheartedly.' "

"I know the Law."

"She doesn't know the letter of the Law, but she obeys the heart of it. She has repented and made God first in her life."

"Who?" a child said, only to be ignored.

131

Amminadab was not mollified. "We shouldn't have foreigners among us. They bring their foreign gods with them. They bring trouble!"

"I agree," Salmon said quietly. "Foreigners do bring trouble. But they cease being foreigners when they cast off their false gods and worship the Lord God with all their heart, mind, and strength."

Amminadab's eyes flashed again. "And how do you know if they are sincere in what they say? How can you trust a woman who has prostituted herself to other gods — not to mention other men?"

"Who?" another child piped in.

"As our fathers and mothers prostituted themselves to the golden calf?" Salmon said, restraining his own rising anger. "How quick you are to forget our own weaknesses and see those of others who have not had the blessing of God's very Presence."

Setting his nephew aside, Amminadab rose. "You risk us all by saving this woman and her relatives!"

The children looked back and forth, confused and frightened. Salmon looked from them to his older brother. "God has given us Jericho, Brother. I don't know how He'll do it, but He will hand it to us. If Rahab and her relatives survive what is to come, it's because death passed over them just as it passed over us. The red cord hanging —"

"Red is the color of a harlot," Nahshon said.

Feeling attacked from all sides, Salmon refused to withdraw. "Red is the color of blood, the blood of the Passover lamb."

"You are so sure of her, Salmon?"

"Leave it to Leah to ask the gentle question," Amminadab mocked when their sister quietly spoke up.

Salmon faced Amminadab again. "The heart of this woman belongs to the Lord; I'm sure of it. She declared her faith as strongly as Miriam, the sister of Moses, did. And do you not wonder? Of all the thousands in that city, the Lord singled out Rahab for our attention. Why would God do that unless He meant to rescue her?"

Salmon spoke to the children. "The Lord didn't save our people because we were worthy. Look how our fathers and mothers turned away from God! They witnessed the ten plagues; they saw God open the Red Sea! They were still faithless and rebelled. And some of our own people turned away to bow down to the baals of Moab. No, we are not worthy. Only the Lord is righteous. No other but the Lord is worthy of praise."

"And yet, God saved *us*," Amminadab said firmly.

Salmon rose and faced the others. "Yes, God saved us. The Lord delivered us because of *His* great mercy. *He* plucked us out of Egypt just as *He* will pluck Rahab out of Jericho. This night we must remember *the Lord our God* freed us. *The Lord* delivered us. *The Lord* redeemed us. *The Lord* took us to be His people. Our salvation depends not on who we are but on who *He* is."

"Who's Rahab?" the children persisted.

"No one important, dear ones," one of the women said softly.

"Just an Amorite woman in Jericho," Nahshon said.

Salmon restrained his anger. "Rahab is a woman of faith. She hid Ephraim and me when the king of Jericho sent his soldiers to capture us. She told us that the Lord our God has given us the city." He smiled at the children and at his sister. "And you'll meet her soon."

"God willing," Amminadab said.

Rahab looked out at the plains of Jericho, where thousands of campfires flickered beneath the starry night. Jobab came and stood beside her. "What is that sound?"

"Singing."

"They're celebrating as though they're already victorious."

"They *are* victorious. Their God is on their side." And soon, she hoped, soon, she and her relatives would be with them, aligned with the Lord God of heaven and earth.

"Why do you think they wait?"

"I don't know. Perhaps their God told them to wait."

"Why?"

"I can't answer, Brother. I'm in the darkness as much as you."

"Maybe they've changed their minds now that they've seen the height and breadth of the city walls," Mizraim said from across the room, where he had been dozing against some cushions.

"They will do to Jericho what they've done to the other Amorite cities," Rahab said, "but the men who came here will rescue us."

"I'm hungry," Bosem whined.

Smiling, Rahab stepped down from the block. "I'll make bread." She added small pieces of wood to the hot coals in the brazier and put the sheet of metal over the top. She and her sisters had ground flour that morning. She poured some into a bowl, added water and seasoning, and worked the dough.

"I hope it will be as you say, Rahab," Mizraim said. "I hope we will be saved."

"God will hold them to their oath." She flattened a piece of dough and turned it round and round until it was thin. She laid it carefully on the hot metal. The dough bubbled and steamed. Using a pronged stick, she watched it briefly and then turned it over carefully. Her house filled with the aroma of roasting grain.

Awbeeb squatted beside her, watching her cook.

"The bread will be ready shortly, little one. Why don't you ask your father to pour wine?"

By the time the first loaf of flat bread was made, she had prepared another to cook. She placed the first on a reed mat to cool and began a third. Her father broke off a piece and passed it to his eldest son. The men ate first, then the children. Rahab broke a round of flat bread into quarters for her sisters. There was enough dough left in the clay bowl to make one small portion of unleavened bread for herself.

Mizraim replenished his father's cup of wine. "Maybe they'll simply wait until we run out of food and water."

"That will take months!" Jobab said. "They're probably looking for a way to break through the gate or set fire to it."

"They won't be able to get close. The king has archers on the wall."

"You still don't understand," Rahab said. "Do you think God will waste the lives of those who honor Him? The God of Israel isn't like the gods of Canaan. He protects His people. He doesn't demand their blood. You waste your time worrying."

Mizraim ignored her. "When the battle begins, there will be confusion."

"Confusion *within* the city, Brother," she said hotly. "There's no confusion out there. They are calm. God is making them ready for battle."

"Why must you go on and on about their god?" her mother cried out.

"There must be something we can do," Jobab said. "Perhaps we should try to get out of the city now, before the battle begins."

"We will wait, as we were told to do," Rahab said, frustrated. "If we try to protect ourselves by our own means, we're doomed right along with everyone else in this city. No. We will trust in the men of God. They will see the red cord and remember their oath. Inside this house, we are safe." She broke off a piece of her bread. Dipping it into the wine, she ate it.

Still, her brothers grumbled and whined and worried. Why did men have such difficulty with inaction? She tried to be patient. She tried to be compassionate. Her father and brothers had been cooped up in this house for days. They were beginning to wear on one another. The women were no better. All this talk of war disturbed them. As much as Rahab loved her relatives, they were a trial to her. No matter how many times she reminded them of the promise and encouraged them, they kept worrying over the future. They were like dogs chewing a bone.

"Why don't we eat our bread and go to sleep?" she suggested. "Let tomorrow take care of itself." She needed some peace and quiet.

When everyone was settled for the night, Rahab went back to the window. With a sigh of contentment, she propped her chin in her palms and watched the Israelite encampment. The night was so still; it was as though everyone and everything around Jericho waited for the Israelites to move forward into battle. She ran her hand over the thick red rope that hung from her window. After a long while, she lay upon her mat. She put her arm across her eyes, fighting her tears.

Come, Lord of heaven and earth! Please come! Break down the gates and take the city! Send Your men to rescue us from this place of desolation! Oh, God of all creation, I'm begging You for mercy. Let the day of our deliverance dawn!

When the battle was won, would the Hebrews allow her to become part of their nation? Ephraim had been far from friendly, quick to judge her. If her future were left up to men like him, what hope had she? He would keep his promise to save her and her family, but that would be the end of his obligations. And she hoped for so much more. Should she have asked for more? begged for more? She would drive herself mad worrying about it. All she could do was wait . . . and hope that God was more merciful than the men who followed Him.

She rose first in the morning as she always did, eager to see if there was any movement in the Israelite camp. She stepped over Mizraim and Basemath and around Vaheb and Hagri. The stars still shone, only the hint of dawn coming.

Startled, she saw an old man of regal bearing standing within arrow shot of the city wall. He was staring up at it. Who was this man dressed for battle, all alone, seemingly without fear of the danger in which he had put himself? Was he studying the walls to find some weakness? He had the bearing of a leader, a man diligent and responsible. Was he contemplating the defenses of the enemy? Surely, if this was the Israelite commander, he should have soldiers with him to act as his bodyguards. Lifting her head, Rahab looked for others who might be keeping watch over this man, but all was quiet in the camp behind him.

When she looked at the man again, another was with him, a soldier, his sword drawn. Where had he come from? Surely she would have seen his approach. The old man went to the soldier quickly, his manner both challenging and eager. He was close enough to the walls of Jericho that she could see his lips move.

Rahab's heart pounded as the old warrior fell to his knees and then prostrated himself before the soldier. Then he rose just enough to remove his sandals! Her skin prickled strangely. Who was the man standing before the elder? Why would the elder bow down to the younger?

Mizraim groaned behind her and rolled over, startling her. She glanced back.

"Mizraim," she said softly. "Get up! Quickly!" She motioned to him frantically.

"Come see what is happening outside the walls!"

When she turned back, the soldier was gone and the old man was striding back toward the Israelite camp, head high, shoulders back. She felt a shiver run through her body.

"What is it?" Mizraim said sleepily, standing beside her, looking out the window as dawn spilled light across the plains of Jericho.

Rahab leaned out the window as far as she could. The soldier was nowhere to be seen. She felt a strange excitement rush through her blood. "The day has come, Mizraim. God is bringing His people into their land!"

Six

"The commander of the Lord's army has given me the Lord's instructions," Joshua called out to the throng of Israelite men of war. He'd already gathered the priests and stretched out his arm toward them. "Take up the Ark of the Covenant, and assign seven priests to walk in front of it, each carrying a ram's horn." He faced the men of war again. "March around the city, and the armed men will lead the way in front of the Ark of the Lord."

Salmon was troubled, as were others around him. They all began talking in low voices. Shouldn't they dig trenches? Shouldn't they erect earthworks? How could they break down the gates of Jericho without a battering ram?

Joshua raised his hands, and the men fell silent again. "Furthermore, do not shout; do not even talk. Not a single word from any of you until I tell you to shout!"

A fast of silence.

The tribes formed ranks, and the captains of hundreds repeated the orders. Then all fell silent again as the vast army started out in obedience to the Lord's command. The only noise Israel made was the rhythmic pounding of marching feet, accompanied by the sounding of the rams' horns.

Rahab heard the king's soldiers shouting from the watchtower on either side of the gate. *"They're coming! The Israelites are coming!"* Footsteps pounded across her roof as soldiers took their duty stations along the wall.

Mizraim flew to the window. "What do we do? Do we wave the red cord? Do we — ?"

"We wait," Rahab said calmly, watching the massive Israelite army marching across the Jericho plain. They were coming straight for the city. The deep, resonant sound of the rams' horns came from the distance, but it was the sound of thousands of marching feet that made her heart quicken. *Thump, thump, thump.* . . . On they came, thousands upon thousands. Closer and closer. *Thump, thump, thump.* She could feel the earth tremble beneath her. Or was it her own ecstatic fear that this was the day the Lord would come? She saw the priests with rams' horns, the Ark of the Lord, and the marching soldiers coming toward her.

"Is that their god?" Mizraim said, standing beside her. "Is it?"

She had never seen anything so beautiful as this object with its strange winged creatures facing one another on the top. "The God who created the heavens and the earth cannot be kept in a box of any size."

"Then what is that thing they carry?"

"I've heard it's called the Ark of the Lord. Their leader, Moses, went up Mount Sinai, and God with His own finger wrote laws upon stone tablets. Surely, that is what they carry."

"If that Ark was captured, would the power pass to others?"

She knew her brother well enough to see where his thinking was taking him. "God chose the Israelites to be His people, and He gave them His laws. I don't know why. But the power isn't contained, Brother. Was it men who struck Egypt with ten plagues or opened the Red Sea? Was it men who rolled up the Jordan like a carpet? Power belongs to the Lord. And the Lord is . . ." She spread her hands, at a loss for words. "The Lord *is*."

"They don't have any battering rams,"

Jobab said, looking over her shoulder.

"Or siege works," her father said as he approached the window.

The men were crowding her, pushing her aside in their eagerness to see the advancing army. And they saw it with men's eyes.

"How do they expect to break down the gates and get into the city?" Mizraim said.

"They will rush the walls soon," her father said grimly. "They're close."

"Almost close enough for the soldiers on the walls to shoot them with arrows," Jobab said.

The first ranks of the Israelite soldiers turned in formation and continued marching along the wall.

"What are they doing?" Mizraim said.

"Maybe they intend to attack from the other side," her father said with a frown.

All morning, they watched as soldiers marched past the window. When the Ark came back around, Rahab closed her eyes and lowered her head in respect as the last of the long phalanx snaked around Jericho.

"They're leaving! The Israelites are leaving!" came the cries from the wall as the Israelite army marched back toward the plains of Jericho. The Jerichoan soldiers were shouting and laughing and jeering.

Rahab winced as she heard the insults being flung after the retreating army. Did the men on the wall not know they were debasing those who would conquer them? She wanted to plug her ears as their crude taunts were flung at the God of Israel. She was ashamed of her people, ashamed of their arrogance, ashamed of their disdain toward the almighty God. If her people had possessed any wisdom, they would have sent ambassadors bearing gifts! The king would have gone out and paid homage to the God of Israel! The king and the people would have thrown open their gates and welcomed the King of Glory! Instead, these hardhearted, senseless, proud people had shut up the city and made it a tomb.

"They've left us!" Mizraim said. "The Israelites are going away!" He turned, his face red in anger. "What do you suppose will happen to us now?"

"You were wrong, Rahab!" Jobab focused his fear and disappointment upon her as well. "The walls *are* high enough and strong enough to protect us!"

"If the king ever finds out you hid the spies and lied to his guards, we'll all die for your treason!" Mizraim added.

"And how will he find out unless one of us tells him?" her father said, now afraid of the king. "Listen to me, all of you. You will keep this to yourselves for the sake of your sister! She thought she was saving your lives!"

Gerah lifted one of her children. "We've been locked up in this house for days, all for nothing!"

Rahab refused to admit she was disappointed. She'd hoped today would be the day of their deliverance, but it seemed God had another plan. She was certain of only one thing. "The walls will not stand against them."

"You said they would come today!"

"They did come today, Basemath," she said quietly, "and I've no doubt they'll come back again tomorrow." She spread her hands. "Don't ask me why it's being done this way. I don't know. Am I God? I can only guess." Why was she saddled with these rebellious people?

"What do you guess?" her mother asked.

Rahab turned to comfort her, for her mother had wept at the sound of those marching feet and now sat distressed and watching her children argue among themselves. "I believe something strange and wonderful will happen here, just as it happened in Egypt and at the Red Sea and at the Jordan only days ago. I'm certain of it, Mother." She looked at the others. "I'm so certain. Haven't I staked my life on Him?"

"And ours," Mizraim said grimly.

Why couldn't her family see God as she did? Did they have scales over their eyes and plugs in their ears? "Yes, I've staked your lives as well. I admit it. But you're still free to choose. You're free to be like the others outside my door who've put their faith in walls instead of the living God. As for me, I'd rather wait and watch and see what God will do. I will stay here. We have been *promised* salvation if we remain in this house!"

"But Rahab," Jobab said, "they can't succeed. They don't even have battering rams!"

How soon men forget! She threw her hands into the air. "Did they need *rafts* to cross the Jordan River?" Calming herself, she continued, "Just wait, my beloved ones. Be patient. Be *still!* Soon you will see and know that God is master of this city and all the land beyond it. The world is His, if He chooses to lay claim to it. And there is nothing anyone in this city can do to stop Him."

"I believe," Awbeeb said.

Laughing, Rahab held her arms out to the child and he leaped into them. "May the others be as wise, my sweet." She settled him on her hip and stepped up to keep watch at the window.

Salmon entered his tent, dismayed at how tired he was. Surely marching a few miles shouldn't deplete him so much. He knelt and prayed silently, thanking God he hadn't needed to fight today. He doubted he would have had the strength to raise a sword. He winced as he lay down. The scar of his circumcision was not fully healed. Or was he merely weary from the inactive days of the Passover celebration?

The camp was silent.

Stretching out on his bed, Salmon frowned as he crossed his arms beneath his head. He wondered what Rahab was doing right now. Had she convinced all her relatives to enter her house and stay there? What if someone had seen her lowering two men from her window? The king could have had her executed by now. Salmon's stomach tightened at the thought, but he forced himself to relax. Surely God would protect a woman who had not only professed, but had also proven, her faith in Him. Salmon had been shaken by her physical beauty when she'd hung boldly out her window and called down to him, but even that did not compare with the courage and conviction she displayed when she put her life at risk to save him and Ephraim. Faith and courage.

He had to get his mind off Rahab.

The silence surrounded him, pressing in upon him until it rang in his ears. What better way to end grumbling, questioning, and discussion than by imposing a fast of silence? The Lord God knew the tendencies of His people. It seemed the inclination of all men and women to question and argue and rebel against any command. The rumble of it had begun before the words of command were fully out of Joshua's mouth.

His father and mother were dead in the wilderness because their generation had rebelled against the Lord. Joshua was wise. Keep the people silent. They became impatient too quickly, thinking they could march in and take the land by themselves. Once before, they'd made that devastating mistake.

Oh, Lord, I look at those massive walls and tremble. How many of us will die when we charge them and batter down the gates to do battle against that evil city? We'll be easy targets for those soldiers on the wall. Will I die before I'm able to fulfill my promise to Rahab?

Drowsy with exhaustion, he closed his eyes. He could still hear the echoes of marching feet in his head. Hour upon hour, mile upon mile. As they had turned away from Jericho, he'd heard taunts and smarted at the insults shouted from the wall. But he'd clenched his teeth and kept marching back to Gilgal.

Is this the reason for Your strange plan, Lord? To humble us? Are You teaching us again to wait upon You? Whether we succeed or fail doesn't depend upon our efforts but upon Your power. Is that what You're trying to get into our thick skulls and hardened hearts?

No answer came.

When Salmon arose the next morning, he fell in among the armed men of Judah as they took their position among the tribes of Israel. The day's order had been passed down from Joshua and disclosed by the captains of hundreds.

The armed warriors of Reuben, Gad, and the half-tribe of Manasseh led the phalanx across the plains of Jericho, followed by the tribes of war-ready men, some priests blowing the rams' horns and others carrying the Ark of the Covenant. They marched around Jericho once and returned to Gilgal, just as they had done the day before.

The orders stood on the third day . . . and the fourth.

Each day the taunts from the soldiers and people on the walls of Jericho grew worse, as they mocked God and laughed and shouted insults. With each circumference, Salmon glanced at the wall and saw the crimson cord hanging from a window in the wall — Rahab's house. Twice he saw someone framed in the window, but the person didn't lean out so that he could see if it was Rahab or one of her relatives. But he knew she was there. The crimson cord told him she was safe. *God, protect her when the battle begins.*

Salmon knew wrath was being stored up in the hearts of his countrymen marching around the city with their shoulders back and their heads held high. His own heart burned within him.

With increasing determination, the people obeyed. They kept silent. They picked up their feet and set them down firmly upon the earth, waiting for the Lord's day of retribution. When it came, they'd be unleashed with swords in hand.

By the fifth day, Salmon was in full strength. The army of Israel was fully healed, rested, conditioned . . . and ready to annihilate those who were blaspheming the Lord God.

"I can still hear them marching," Basemath said after the Israelite army had marched around the city, then left, for the sixth time. "My head is pounding with the sound of it. All those thousands of men and their pounding feet."

"It seemed louder today than yesterday," Gerah said.

"Every time the Israelites march around the city, the earth seems to tremble a little more. Can you feel it?" Zebach said. "Or am I imagining things?"

Rahab watched Mizraim run his hand over a wooden cabinet that was covered with dust that hadn't been there at dawn, when the Israelites began marching around the city. He rubbed his fingers together and then brushed his hands off. Frowning, he looked around at the ceiling and the walls. "There's a crack in the wall by the door." He glanced at her.

She smiled tightly. "Perhaps tomorrow will be the day of our deliverance, Mizraim. Maybe tomorrow we'll be free, with no walls around us." Not even those of their old way of thinking.

At dawn on the seventh day, the Sabbath day that belonged to the Lord, the marching orders changed. Salmon breathed hard, for it took all his strength to keep still and silent and not raise his fists in the air in exultation. His heart pounded a battle beat as he and the multitude of his brethren maintained discipline.

Today, the battle would begin. Today, he would fight his way into the city, find Rahab, and get her and her family to safety before destruction came upon them.

For today, *Jericho would fall!*

Seven

"They're not leaving this time," Mizraim said, standing at the window. "They're going around the city again!"

Jobab joined him, leaning past Mizraim to see for himself. "It's true!"

Rahab checked the water supply. Satisfied there was plenty, she filled a bowl and motioned for Awbeeb. "We must get ready." She soaked a piece of linen and wrung it out. "We want to look our best when they come for us." She washed Awbeeb's dusty face.

He winced as she cleaned his ears. "Will they come soon?"

"We will be ready and hope this is the day the Lord has chosen."

"How will the soldiers get into the city?"

"The Lord their God will let them in. Now go and ask your mother if she has a fresh tunic for you. Bosem, come and wash your face and hands." She glanced at her mother and sisters, who sat staring at her. She couldn't suppress the excitement and joy she felt bubbling up inside her. "Get up! Wash yourselves! Brush your hair. Let's dress in the best we have! Should we greet those who deliver us with dour, dusty faces and dirty clothing?" She laughed. "We will dress as though we are attending a wedding!" She opened her cabinets and took out robes she had purchased over the years. "Today all Canaan will see that walls cannot prevail against the Lord our God. Today is the day of our deliverance!"

Someone moaned. "That's what you said yesterday."

"And the day before," another added.

Three times the Israelites marched around the city. Then a fourth, and a fifth, and a sixth. It seemed each time Salmon rounded the city, his strength grew, for it was the day of the Lord, and the Lord would take the day. The red cord hung from a window not far from the east gate. Salmon fixed his eyes upon it as he headed around the city for the seventh time, Ephraim marching beside him.

Then the command came. Joshua called out, "Shout! For the Lord has given you the city! The city and everything in it must be completely destroyed as an offering to the Lord. Only Rahab the prostitute and the others in her house will be spared, for she protected our spies. Do not take any of the things set apart for destruction, or you yourselves will be completely destroyed, and you will bring trouble on all Israel. Everything made from silver, gold, bronze, or iron is sacred to the Lord and must be brought into His treasury."

As the seventh round began, Salmon's heart beat harder and faster. His feet came down more firmly, joining the thousands of others so that the sound of Israel marching seemed to reverberate against the mountains to the west.

Then the massive army stopped and faced the city. The horns sounded their blast, joined by a million voices in a ferocious battle cry.

Rahab's heart trembled at the horrifying sound. As a low rumble sounded, she heard screaming from the men in the gate tower, and she clutched the windowsill as everything around her shook. Screams of terror followed from her mother and sisters, and even her father and brothers were shouting, "The walls!"

Dust billowed up as stones broke loose

and tumbled down. An entire section of the wall between her house and the gate was collapsing, stones pouring in an avalanche onto the roadway. Men and women spilled out and were crushed beneath the crumbling fortress.

Then the Israelites broke ranks and came running, their battle cry raising the hair on the back of her neck. Thousands raced toward her, swords drawn and raised. Some who had fallen from the walls were wounded and tried to rise. They were cut down by the first line of Israelites.

Rahab jumped down from the step by the window. "Gather your possessions. We must be ready when our rescuers get here! Quickly, Basemath! Children, stand behind me!" She stepped forward as the screaming of the Israelites grew louder. The outer wall of her house cracked, one section breaking free. "All of you, stand behind me. Quickly!" she cried out above the din. "Don't be afraid! Stand firm!"

"Keep your promise!" Joshua shouted to Salmon and Ephraim as they all ran. "Go to the prostitute's house and bring her out, along with all her family!"

Zeal for the Lord swelled in Salmon until his blood was a fire within him, retribution in his hand. Screaming the battle cry, he ran with all the pent-up rage from days of listening to insults and blasphemies shouted from the battlements. He looked neither to the right nor the left, but ran straight toward the fallen gate, leaping onto it. Swinging his sword, Salmon cut down a Jerichoan soldier who was clamoring to get out of the path of the avenging army of God.

"This way!" Salmon shouted above the din of enraged soldiers and terrified foes. "This way, Ephraim!"

They turned to the right, running along the street down which Rahab had taken them the day they first entered the city. Israelite soldiers by the thousands were pouring over the collapsed walls while Jerichoans fought in confusion, their voices a babel of terror and chaos. Salmon parried a blow and brought his sword down and around, so that the attacker's weapon flew out of his hand. Slicing through him, Salmon freed his sword and ran on.

There were screams all around him as the vanquished fell before the swords of the victors. "Rahab!" he shouted, racing past the crumbled houses containing their crushed inhabitants. Where was she? One portion of the wall of her house was still standing, though parts of it were crumbling into the street. *"Rahab!"*

"We're here!"

His heart did a strange flip at the sound of her voice. The door of her house lay split in two in the stone-strewn street. Salmon entered the open section of her wall and found her standing in the middle of the house, more than a dozen others behind her. Her arms were outstretched, as if to shield her family. Her lovely face was pale, but her eyes were bright. Ephraim ran in behind him.

Rahab inclined her head in greeting and respect. "Welcome!"

Lowering his sword, Salmon stepped forward and extended his hand. "Come with me." Her fingers were cool when she took his hand. Studying her, he saw the pulse beating wildly in her throat. She was not as calm as she appeared. "You are safe now, Rahab. We'll get you out of here." He drew her toward the gaping doorway.

"If you want to live, follow us!" Ephraim said to the others behind them.

Rahab felt the heat rush into her face as the young man separated her from her family. She looked back and extended her hand toward them, then saw that her father, mother, brothers and sisters, and their children were obeying Ephraim's command, and he was taking up a protective position behind them.

Across the street, a fire blazed. The bodies of her neighbors lay in their doorways. Screams came from the center of the city. She could hear stones cascading into the street behind her. When she glanced back, she saw her house collapsing.

Salmon released her hand and caught her around the waist. "This way," he said sternly, urging her forward. "Hurry!" He lifted her over some rubble. Over his shoulder, she saw her relatives hastening after them.

When Salmon turned to help the others, Rahab held her arms out to Awbeeb. He scrambled over some fallen rocks, and she caught him up into her arms. Awbeeb clung to her, his face buried in her neck. Everywhere she looked, there was carnage. They picked their way hurriedly through the crumbled wall. She looked back at the others. "Keep going, Rahab!" Salmon commanded her. "Don't look back! We'll see to the others. Now go! Wait for us beneath the palms."

When Rahab reached the outer edge of the rubble, she ran. She didn't stop until she reached the shade of the palms. She set

Awbeeb on his feet and turned to encourage the others. Dragging air into her burning lungs, she called out to her mother and sisters, who were running from the rubble with the rest of the children. Her father and brothers came more slowly, heavily burdened with family possessions. Salmon and Ephraim brought up the rear, swords drawn and ready to protect them if need be.

Her mother's face was ashen as Rahab helped her sit against the palm. Basemath, Gowlan, and Gerah were weeping and holding their children close. Hagri was blinking back tears and staring back toward the city. Rahab followed her gaze.

Jericho looked as though a hand had come down from heaven and flattened it against the earth. The walls and towers were scattered stones that had collapsed and rolled outward. Screams still rent the air as smoke and fire rose.

"This way," Salmon said, grasping her arm. He turned her toward the Israelite encampment at Gilgal.

By sunset, the once great trading center of Jericho was burning. The air was acrid, smoke billowing into the darkening sky. Red and orange tongues of fire licked up the last bits of wooden rubble within the circle of tumbled stone. The cloying scent of burning flesh was heavy.

Shuddering, Rahab clasped her knees to her chest. She was weary with exhaustion, greatly relieved to have survived the destruction and yet saddened as well. All those thousands of people were now dead because they'd foolishly put their trust in man-made walls rather than in the living God who had created the stones. They'd heard the stories just as she had. Why had they refused to believe?

Salmon and Ephraim guarded her and her family as the Israelites returned from battle.

"None of your men are carrying any plunder," Mizraim said in surprise.

"Jericho is accursed," Ephraim said.

Salmon seemed more hospitable and willing to explain. "The Lord commanded through Joshua that every living thing in the city was to be killed: man, woman, child — young and old, ox, sheep, and donkey. Whatever silver, gold, brass, or iron that remains after the fire will be brought into the Lord's treasury. We take nothing for ourselves."

Rahab lowered her head against her knees. She didn't want Salmon or Ephraim to see her tears. They might misunderstand and think she grieved over the fallen city or that she wasn't grateful that they had fulfilled their vow. Her heart was filled with thanksgiving toward the Lord God of heaven and earth, who had held these men to their promise. She and every member of her family were alive and safe.

Yet she had hoped for more. Oh, so much more.

Someone gripped her shoulder. She glanced up sharply to see her brother Jobab bending over her. "I'm sorry I ever doubted you, Rahab."

"I, as well," said Mizraim. "The god of the Hebrews is a mighty god, indeed." He sat with his wife and children, putting his arms around them and holding them close.

The last of the Israelites returned to Gilgal.

"You will be safe here," Salmon said. He inclined his head to Rahab and then turned and walked away. Ephraim went with him.

Rahab rose quickly and followed to the edge of darkness. She stopped there and watched the two young men head back to the Israelite encampment. Behind her, no one said anything. When the two men disappeared among the tents of Israel, Rahab closed her eyes and fought despair.

After a long while, her father came out to her and put his arm around her shoulders.

"We are all relieved, my daughter. Because of your wisdom, we are alive and safe."

She lowered her hands angrily. "We are all alive because of God." Tears coursed down her cheeks.

"Yes, of course."

Cautious words, not faithful ones. Rahab shook her head sadly. None of those she loved would understand her sorrow. Even now, after all they'd heard and seen, they didn't share her faith or the desire of her heart. Nor would they understand her desolation. She was unworthy to be counted among the Israelites. God had rescued her from destruction. He had shown mercy upon her and her family members. But that didn't mean she was acceptable in His sight. That didn't mean she could assume a place among His people. She saw in the faces of the men who had come to represent their people that she was still just "the harlot from Jericho."

Her shoulders shook, and she covered her mouth to hold back the sobs.

"Do you cry for those who died, Rahab?"

"No," she said raggedly.

She wept because her dream of being a follower of the true God was turning to dust. She was still outside the

165

camp of Israel.

Rahab slept fitfully that night and rose early in the morning. She stood in the predawn twilight, watching the Israelite camp awaken. As the sun rose, three men approached. Her heart leapt, and she immediately awakened the others. They all rose quickly and stood with her. Rahab moved to stand beside her father.

She recognized Salmon and Ephraim immediately, but not the older man with them, who walked with grave dignity. She and her family members bowed down before them.

"It is *him,*" her father said quietly. "The man I met in the palm grove forty years ago!" He knelt and put the palms of his hands and his forehead to the earth. "I would recognize him anywhere."

It was the man she'd seen studying the walls before the march began, the man who had bowed down to the soldier with the drawn sword.

"Arise!" the elderly man said, hitting his staff against the ground. "Bow down before God, not man."

Rahab rose quickly and helped her father to his feet. She could feel how he was shaking. And no wonder, for when she looked into the commander's eyes, she trembled as well. Never had she seen such fierceness in a human face.

"I am Joshua."

"You and I met once many years ago in the palm grove," her father said. "I knew you would return."

"I remember you, Abiasaph."

Her father bowed his head again. "I thank you for taking pity upon my family and sparing our lives."

"It is God who has rescued you from destruction, Abiasaph, not I," Joshua said. "But now it is left to you to decide what you will do with the lives you've been given. Have you considered your future?"

"Our only desire is to live."

"Your lives are granted you," Joshua said. "No one in Israel will do you harm. Where do you wish to go?"

"If it is as you say and we can decide for ourselves," her father continued cautiously, "then I would ask that we be allowed to return to the palm grove so that we might live there safely and make a living for ourselves."

Heart sinking, Rahab closed her eyes.

Joshua inclined his head in agreement. "You may go, Abiasaph, you and yours, and peace be with you!"

Afraid he would leave and she would never

have another opportunity to speak for herself, Rahab stepped forward. "I don't wish to go!" All eyes focused upon her — her father's and brothers' in warning, her mother's and sisters' in fear.

Salmon's eyes glowed and he seemed ready to speak on her behalf, but she turned her face from him. She could only imagine what had been said to him for giving his oath to rescue her and her family. She would not risk shaming him now. Besides, her hope rested on no man. Let God be her judge. If He were an eagle and she a mouse scurrying for shelter, she would still seek refuge beneath His mighty wings.

Joshua considered her enigmatically. "You are Rahab, the prostitute who hid our spies."

"I am Rahab."

"What is it you want, woman?"

Her father had chosen for the family, but she had this one chance, this one brief moment when opportunity lay within her grasp.

"Don't be afraid," Joshua said. "Speak."

"I want to become one of the people of God, no matter what it takes."

Joshua turned his head and looked at Salmon. Rahab held her breath, studying the two men. Was Joshua giving Salmon a silent reprimand for sparing her and her relatives and bringing this bother upon him?

Was he blaming the young man for her outrageous plea? She could almost imagine what he was thinking: *How dare this brazen harlot think she deserves to be among God's people! Isn't it enough that the Lord spared her life? What right has she to ask for more? Be off with her!*

"If I cannot be grafted into God's own people, then it would have been better had I died among the rest of those lost souls in Jericho!"

Her father grasped her wrist and gave her a hard jerk. "Be silent, Daughter. Be thankful for your life!"

She yanked free and appealed to Joshua again. "I am thankful to God for my salvation, but you have said we can choose, and so I choose not to go back to my old life. I want to start afresh. Would that I could be a new creation under God!"

Her father said quickly, "She knows not what she says."

"Indeed, she does," Salmon said.

"She is only a woman and foolish," Mizraim said, clearly angry with her, his expression warning her to silence. *This, from a man who would have put his hope in the walls of Jericho and the wooden idols now ash in the rubble,* she thought angrily, refusing to be cowed.

169

Joshua raised his hand for silence. "The Lord has shown pity toward all of you," he said, "but toward this woman, He has shown compassion beyond measure. Abiasaph, your request has been granted. Take your family and go in peace. Live in the palm grove as you wish. But be warned: Jericho is accursed. Any man who rebuilds the city will do so not only at the expense of his firstborn son but of his youngest as well."

"What of my daughter?"

"If Rahab wants to remain behind, she may."

As Joshua and the two spies walked away, her eyes filled with tears. She hung her head in sorrow.

"You see how it is," Mizraim said, while his wife began repacking their possessions. "They think they're better than we are. They don't want a woman like you among them."

She didn't answer. She knew what he said was true, but she refused to let him see her pain.

"We'll build you a house near the road, Rahab," Jobab offered. "You can have a lucrative business —"

"I'm staying here." She sat down.

"Stubborn woman! Show some sense!"

"Sense?" She glared up at him. "What sense is there in walking away from a God who protects His people?"

"He didn't protect *our* people!" Mizraim pointed out, gesturing toward Jericho. "You can still smell their burning flesh on the wind."

"Those are my people," she said and pointed toward Gilgal.

"I want to go home," her mother said, weeping. "When can we go back to our house in the grove?"

"Will you go back to worshiping your little wooden idols as well?" Rahab asked bitterly.

"The god who destroyed Jericho isn't for us," her father said gravely. "We're alive, and that's all that matters."

"No, Father. It isn't enough to be alive but not serve the God who rescued us."

"Not for you, perhaps," Mizraim said. "But enough for us."

"Then go!"

"Please come with us, Daughter," her mother pleaded. "What will become of you if you stay behind? The Israelites will never allow you to live among them."

"I'll make her come," Mizraim said angrily, reaching for her.

She slapped his hand away. "I've had stronger men than you try to bend me to their will! Don't try it!"

"Leave her alone," her father said, hefting

a bundle onto his back. "Give her a few days to think things over. She'll come to her senses."

"When will you come to yours?" she cried out. "How can you turn away after you've seen the truth?"

"What truth?" Jobab said.

That it was God who saved you!

"It was you, Rahab," her father said. "And we're grateful."

"But you all know the stories about God just as I do. Haven't I told you each and every one as I heard it?"

"Yes, this god has great power."

"*All* power!"

"All the more reason to go, my dear. Such a god is best avoided."

"And how do you propose to do that, Father? Where can you hide from Him?"

He looked troubled, but remained firm. "We will dwell quietly among the palms as Joshua has said we can. We will go about our business and not interfere with theirs. And, in this way, we will have peace with the people of Israel and their god."

Shaking her head, she looked away toward the Israelite encampment of Gilgal and wept.

"Come with us," Hagri said. "Please, Sister. You'll be all alone here."

"I'm staying."

"And if they break camp and leave?"

"I'll follow."

"Why?"

"Because I have to." How could she explain that she yearned for God, like a deer panting for water?

Crying softly, Hagri kissed Rahab on the head and then walked away.

Salmon stood with Joshua at the edge of the encampment. "I told you she wouldn't go with them."

"Leave her alone for three days. Give her time to consider her choices. If she remains, you may go and bring her in among the tents of Israel."

"She is a woman alone. Shouldn't a guard be posted?"

Joshua smiled at him. "She already has one."

As the sun rose on the fourth day of her solitude, Rahab saw a man walking toward her. It was Salmon. He was unsmiling as he came near, and she wondered what dour message he had to give her. Perhaps Joshua had sent him to warn her away.

"You've remained here for three days," he

said, standing on the opposite side of her fire.

"Joshua said I was free to choose, and I choose to stay here." She poked the fire. She had enough grain to make bread for today only; tomorrow she'd go hungry.

"How long do you plan to stay here?"

"As long as Israel remains in Gilgal."

"We will be moving soon."

"Then I suppose I'll be moving, too."

He straightened, and she thought he would walk away. "I will take you into my tent and cover you with my mantle."

Her face went hot at his proposal of marriage. "You?" She covered her cheeks with her hands.

He frowned slightly. "You refuse?"

"You're so young!"

He grinned. "I'm old enough."

She gave a bitter laugh. "Marriage to someone like me? You don't know what you're saying. Didn't you hear Joshua the other day? I am Rahab *the prostitute,* a prostitute in the eyes of all Israel and anyone else who hears of me."

"Ah, yes, the woman with a past to whom God has given a future."

"Do not jest about such things," she said angrily, struggling against the tears. If only she could live her life over, she would change so many things.

"I do not jest, Rahab." He came around the fire. Reaching down, he took her hand, drawing her firmly to her feet. "Why do you suppose Ephraim and I came into Jericho?"

"To spy out the city."

"So we were told."

"So you *said.*" Frowning, she looked up at him.

"So we thought, but I've been wondering ever since I met you."

He had the most beautiful, tender brown eyes. "Wondering what?" When he touched her cheek lightly, her heart quickened.

"If God didn't send us to find you."

"Why would God take note of an unworthy woman like me?"

"Because the Lord knows His people wherever they are, even when they're inside the walls of a pagan city. He knew *you,* Rahab, and He answered the prayer of your heart. God saved you from death, and God is now offering you a way to be grafted into His people."

She shook her head and stepped back from him. As much as the idea might appeal to her, this would not do at all. "I know God is my Savior. I also know He is God of all there is and thus master of my life."

"Then accept the blessing He offers you."

Salmon smiled and placed his hand against his heart. "A young husband."

She laughed bleakly. "Young and impulsive." Jerking free, she turned away. "Give yourself a few days, and you'll be glad I said no."

"I made up my mind the day I met you."

She turned back and arched a brow at him. "Oh, really?" How many times had she heard such nonsense? The king of Jericho had said such words to her. "When did you know, Salmon? When I was hanging out the window and brazenly calling out to you?" She touched her hair. "Was it my streaming black tresses that set your heart afire?" She touched her throat. "Or my other 'character attributes'?" Her fingers teased the neckline of her dress.

His eyes never left hers. "When I first looked up at you in the wall of Jericho, I saw you as a harlot. Bold. Filled with iniquity. But when I came into your house and you spoke to us, I saw you for what you are — a woman of wisdom, a woman worthy of praise."

"Oh, Salmon . . ." When she started to turn away, he caught hold of her and turned her around to face him.

"Almost from the moment you proclaimed

your faith in God, I loved you."

"Love?"

"Yes, *love*. In all my life, I haven't met a woman among all Israel who is more worthy of praise than you. All the young women I know have seen the pillar of fire, the cloud that rises and leads us across the desert wasteland. They have drunk water that streamed from a rock and eaten manna from heaven. And still their faith does not match yours. From you will come prophets . . . perhaps even the Messiah."

"Messiah?" What did the word mean?

He smiled again. "There is so much to teach you, so many things you don't know. The history of our people, the Law, the promises of God . . ." He cupped her face tenderly. "Be my wife, and I will teach you."

"And what will your family say?"

"That I am prudent in selecting such a wife. Caleb has already given permission."

"Who is Caleb?"

"Leader over my tribe, the tribe of Judah. He was with Joshua when Moses sent men to spy out Canaan forty years ago. He and Joshua are the only two survivors from my father's generation. Caleb is held in high esteem by all." His mouth tipped wryly as he ran one hand over her hair. "He suggested that he be the one to marry you, but I told him he already had one wife too many."

She swallowed back her tears, amazed at the mercy of God. First He rescued her, and now it seemed He was providing a man of God to be her husband. Her *husband!* Never had she dreamed of such a thing.

"You are the woman I've waited for," Salmon said quietly. "Come with me."

She put her hand up so he would know she needed a moment. She couldn't speak a word past the lump in her throat. He frowned, dismayed, and she knew she had to show him she had decided. Stepping away from him, she knelt and scooped dirt over her fire. Gathering her possessions into a bundle, she straightened, tears of joy trickling down her cheeks.

Smiling once more, Salmon stepped forward and wiped them away. If she had doubted his words of love before, she did no longer, for his gaze shone with the joy of someone who had just been given exactly what he wanted.

Salmon picked up her bundle, took her by the hand, and led her home.

EPILOGUE

Rahab and Salmon had a son, Boaz.
Boaz was the father of Obed;
Obed, the father of Jesse;
Jesse, the father of King David.
And from the line of King David of the
   tribe of Judah
came the promised Messiah,
Jesus Christ our Savior and Lord.

SEEK AND FIND

DEAR READER,

You have just read the story of Rahab as perceived by one author. Is this the whole truth about the story of Rahab and the fall of Jericho? Jesus said to seek and you will find the answers you need for life. The best way to find the truth is to look for yourself!

This "Seek and Find" section is designed to help you discover the story of Rahab as recorded in the Bible. It consists of six short studies that you can do on your own or with a small discussion group.

You may be surprised to learn that this ancient story will have applications for your life today. No matter where we live or in what century, God's Word is truth. It is as relevant today as it was yesterday. In it we find a future and a hope.

Peggy Lynch

THE VISIT

Read the following passage:

Then Joshua secretly sent out two spies from the Israelite camp at Acacia. He instructed them, "Spy out the land on the other side of the Jordan River, especially around Jericho." So the two men set out and came to the house of a prostitute named Rahab and stayed there that night.

But someone told the king of Jericho, "Some Israelites have come here tonight to spy out the land." So the king of Jericho sent orders to Rahab: "Bring out the men who have come into your house. They are spies sent here to discover the best way to attack us."

Rahab, who had hidden the two men, replied, "The men were here earlier, but I didn't know where they were from. They left the city at dusk, as the city gates were about to close, and I don't know where they went. If you hurry, you can probably catch up with them." (But she had taken them up to the roof and hidden them beneath piles of flax.) So the king's men went looking for the spies along the road leading to the shallow crossing places of the Jordan River. And as soon as the king's men had left, the city gate was shut.

Joshua 2:1–7

Joshua secretly sent two men to spy out Jericho. What things in this passage indicate that this mission was not a secret to the citizens of Jericho?

Where did the spies go?

Who is Rahab? How does she make her living?

According to this passage, how did the king of Jericho view these two "visitors"?

How did Rahab perceive these visitors?

Contrast the king's and Rahab's responses to the visitors.

Find God's Ways for You

Most of us will never face an invading army as Rahab did, but we do face overwhelming situations of other kinds. What kinds of problems are you facing right now? What kinds of choices do you have?

Read the following passage:

> If you need wisdom — if you want to know what God wants you to do — ask him, and he will gladly tell you. He will not resent your asking. But when you ask him, be sure that you really expect him to answer, for a doubtful mind is as unsettled as a wave of the sea that is driven and tossed by the wind. People like that should not expect to receive anything from the Lord. They can't make up their minds. They waver back and forth in everything they do.
>
> James 1:5–8

What does this passage tell you to do?

What warning do you find?

Stop and Ponder

How are you wavering in your decisions?

THE STAND

Read the following passage:

Before the spies went to sleep that night, Rahab went up on the roof to talk with them. "I know the Lord has given you this land," she told them. "We are all afraid of you. Everyone is living in terror. For we have heard how the Lord made a dry path for you through the Red Sea when you left Egypt. And we know what you did to Sihon and Og, the two Amorite kings east of the Jordan River, whose people you completely destroyed. No wonder our hearts have melted in fear! No one has the courage to fight after hearing such things. For the Lord your God is the supreme God of the heavens above and the earth below. Now swear to me by the Lord that you will be kind to me and my family since I have helped you. Give me some guarantee that when Jericho is conquered, you will let me live, along with my father and mother, my brothers and sisters, and all their families."

"We offer our own lives as a guarantee for your safety," the men agreed. "If you don't betray us, we will keep our promise when the Lord gives us the land."

Joshua 2:8–14

List the reasons that the people's hearts had melted in fear and no courage remained.

What declaration does Rahab make about God?

What does Rahab ask of the spies?

Rahab asks the men for a promise. Upon whom is that promise based?

How do the spies respond?

FIND GOD'S WAYS FOR YOU
What fears grip you? Why?

What do you do when you are fearful?

What kind of advice have you given to others who are fearful?

King David, one of Rahab's most famous descendants, wrote of God: "Even when I walk through the dark valley of death, I will not be afraid, for you are close beside me. Your rod and your staff protect and comfort me" (Psalm 23:4).

What does God offer you?

STOP AND PONDER
Where is God in relation to you right now?

THE ESCAPE

SEEK GOD'S WORD FOR TRUTH

Read the following passage:

> Then, since Rahab's house was built into the city wall, she let them down by a rope through the window. "Escape to the hill country," she told them. "Hide there for three days until the men who are searching for you have returned; then go on your way."
>
> Before they left, the men told her, "We can guarantee your safety only if you leave this scarlet rope hanging from the window. And all your family members — your father, mother, brothers, and all your relatives — must be here inside the house. If they go out into the street, they will be killed, and we cannot be held to our oath. But we swear that no one inside this house will be killed — not a hand will be laid on

any of them. If you betray us, however, we are not bound by this oath in any way."

"I accept your terms," she replied. And she sent them on their way, leaving the scarlet rope hanging from the window.

The spies went up into the hill country and stayed there three days. The men who were chasing them had searched everywhere along the road, but they finally returned to the city without success. Then the two spies came down from the hill country, crossed the Jordan River, and reported to Joshua all that had happened to them. "The Lord will certainly give us the whole land," they said, "for all the people in the land are terrified of us."

Joshua 2:15–24

Where was Rahab's house located?

How did she help the spies escape?

What instructions did she give the spies? Why?

What warning and conditions of rescue did the spies give Rahab?

What was Rahab's response?

What signal was Rahab to use?

FIND GOD'S WAYS FOR YOU

Like Rahab, we have opportunities to help others. List some ways you have helped others.

What advice have you given?

Jesus said, "Don't worry about having enough food or drink or clothing. Why be like the pagans who are so deeply concerned about these things? Your heavenly Father already knows all your needs" (Matthew 6:31–32).

What instruction and what promise does Jesus offer here? What is the condition?

STOP AND PONDER

Who has first place in your life?

THE WAIT

Read the following passage:

Now the gates of Jericho were tightly shut because the people were afraid of the Israelites. No one was allowed to go in or out. But the Lord said to Joshua, "I have given you Jericho, its king, and all its mighty warriors. Your entire army is to march around the city once a day for six days. Seven priests will walk ahead of the Ark, each carrying a ram's horn. On the seventh day you are to march around the city seven times, with the priests blowing the horns. When you hear the priests give one long blast on the horns, have all the people give a mighty shout. Then the walls of the city will collapse, and the people can charge straight into the city."

So Joshua called together the priests

and said, "Take up the Ark of the Covenant, and assign seven priests to walk in front of it, each carrying a ram's horn." Then he gave orders to the people: "March around the city, and the armed men will lead the way in front of the Ark of the Lord."

After Joshua spoke to the people, the seven priests with the rams' horns started marching in the presence of the Lord, blowing the horns as they marched. And the priests carrying the Ark of the Lord's covenant followed behind them. Armed guards marched both in front of the priests and behind the Ark, with the priests continually blowing the horns. "Do not shout; do not even talk," Joshua commanded. "Not a single word from any of you until I tell you to shout. Then shout!" So the Ark of the Lord was carried around the city once that day, and then everyone returned to spend the night in the camp.

Joshua got up early the next morning, and the priests again carried the Ark of the Lord. The seven priests with the rams' horns marched in front of the Ark of the Lord, blowing their horns. Armed guards marched both in front of the priests with the horns and behind the Ark of the Lord. All this time the priests were sounding their horns. On the second day they marched around the city once and returned to the camp. They followed this pattern for six days.

Joshua 6:1–14

Why was Jericho "tightly shut"?

What proclamation does the Lord give Joshua?

List the battle instructions given by God.

What instructions does Joshua give to the people?

How do the priests and army respond?

Rahab and her family members are also tightly shut up within the walls of Jericho, waiting for the impending battle. They must have been watching from the wall. What indications do you find that no one knew when the day of victory/rescue would be?

FIND GOD'S WAYS FOR YOU

Rahab and her family members were locked up inside her house within the walls of Jericho — waiting for the promised rescue. In what ways are you locked up?

What kind of waiting place are you in?

Psalm 27:14 says: "Wait patiently for the Lord. Be brave and courageous. Yes, wait patiently for the Lord."
What instruction is given in this verse?

What does it mean to you?

STOP AND PONDER
On whom do you rely for strength and courage?

THE RESCUE

Read the following passage:

On the seventh day the Israelites got up at dawn and marched around the city as they had done before. But this time they went around the city seven times. The seventh time around, as the priests sounded the long blast on their horns, Joshua commanded the people, "Shout! For the Lord has given you the city! The city and everything in it must be completely destroyed as an offering to the Lord. Only Rahab the prostitute and the others in her house will be spared, for she protected our spies. Do not take any of the things set apart for destruction, or you yourselves will be completely destroyed, and you will bring trouble on all Israel. Everything made from silver, gold, bronze, or iron is sacred to the Lord and must be brought into his treasury."

When the people heard the sound of the horns, they shouted as loud as they could. Suddenly, the walls of Jericho collapsed, and the Israelites charged straight into the city from every side and captured it. They completely destroyed everything in it — men and women, young and old, cattle, sheep, donkeys — everything.

Then Joshua said to the two spies, "Keep your promise. Go to the prostitute's house and bring her out, along with all her family."

The young men went in and brought out Rahab, her father, mother, brothers, and all the other relatives who were with her. They moved her whole family to a safe place near the camp of Israel.

Then the Israelites burned the city and everything in it. Only the things made from silver, gold, bronze, or iron were kept for the treasury of the Lord's house. So Joshua spared Rahab the prostitute and her relatives who were with her in the house, because she had hidden the spies Joshua sent to Jericho. And she lives among the Israelites to this day.

Joshua 6:15–25

In the previous lesson we learned about the plan during the six days of waiting. What new instructions were carried out on the seventh day?

What instructions were given regarding Rahab?

Whom did Joshua send to rescue Rahab and her family? Where were they taken?

What happened to the city and its contents?

What items were spared and why?

Rahab and her family were spared. What reason is given?

FIND GOD'S WAYS FOR YOU

When your world is falling apart and things are not going as you planned, what do you do to try to regain control?

God says, "My thoughts are completely different from yours. . . . And my ways are far beyond anything you could imagine. For just as the heavens are higher than the earth, so are my ways higher than your ways and

my thoughts higher than your thoughts"
(Isaiah 55:8–9).

What do you learn about God's ways and
thoughts from these verses?

Jesus said, "For God so loved the world
that he gave his only Son, so that everyone
who believes in him will not perish but have
eternal life. God did not send his Son into
the world to condemn it, but to save it"
(John 3:16–17).

What is God's rescue plan for the world?

Why does He want to rescue you?

STOP AND PONDER

Whom have you chosen to rescue you?

THE OUTCOME

Read the following passage:

So Joshua spared Rahab the prostitute and her relatives who were with her in the house, because she had hidden the spies Joshua sent to Jericho. And she lives among the Israelites to this day.

Joshua 6:25

Of those rescued, how many made their home in the midst of Israel?

What reason is given?

The story does not end here. We are not told what happened to Rahab's family members, but we do know what happened to Rahab. She married an Israelite named Salmon and bore him a son. Rahab is considered a woman of great faith, and she is held in high esteem in the Bible. The following passage about Rahab was written centuries after her death:

> What is faith? It is the confident assurance that what we hope for is going to happen. It is the evidence of things we cannot yet see. . . . It was by faith that Rahab the prostitute did not die with all the others in her city who refused to obey God. For she had given a friendly welcome to the spies.
> Hebrews 11:1, 31

Based upon what you've learned about Rahab, how does this definition of faith apply to her?

How did she demonstrate her faith?

The apostle Paul wrote: "God saved you by his special favor when you believed. And you can't take credit for this; it is a gift from God. Salvation is not a reward for the good things we have done, so none of us can boast about it" (Ephesians 2:8–9).
From this, what else do you learn about faith?

The apostle Paul also wrote: "I did this so

that you might trust the power of God rather than human wisdom" (1 Corinthians 2:5).

Upon whom did Rahab base her faith?

And finally, the outcome of Rahab's story is the honor given to her in the first chapter of the Gospel of Matthew, where she is listed in the lineage of Jesus Christ, the Messiah (see pages 161–162).

FIND GOD'S WAYS FOR YOU

Your story does not end here, either. What have you learned about yourself from this study?

What changes, if any, have you made?

How would you describe your relationship with God and why?

How do you choose to live out your life?

STOP AND PONDER

How have God's ways become your ways?

THE GENEALOGY OF JESUS THE CHRIST

This is a record of the ancestors of Jesus the Messiah, a descendant of King David and of Abraham:

Abraham was the father of Isaac.
Isaac was the father of Jacob.
Jacob was the father of Judah and his brothers.
Judah was the father of Perez and Zerah (their mother was **Tamar**).
Perez was the father of Hezron.
Hezron was the father of Ram.
Ram was the father of Amminadab.
Amminadab was the father of Nahshon.
Nahshon was the father of Salmon.
Salmon was the father of Boaz (his mother was **Rahab**).
Boaz was the father of Obed (his mother was **Ruth**).
Obed was the father of Jesse.
Jesse was the father of King David.

David was the father of Solomon (his mother was **Bathsheba**, the widow of Uriah).

Solomon was the father of Rehoboam.

Rehoboam was the father of Abijah.

Abijah was the father of Asaph.

Asaph was the father of Jehoshaphat.

Jehoshaphat was the father of Jehoram.

Jehoram was the father of Uzziah.

Uzziah was the father of Jotham.

Jotham was the father of Ahaz.

Ahaz was the father of Hezekiah.

Hezekiah was the father of Manasseh.

Manasseh was the father of Amos.

Amos was the father of Josiah.

Josiah was the father of Jehoiachin and his brothers (born at the time of the exile to Babylon).

After the Babylonian exile:

Jehoiachin was the father of Shealtiel.

Shealtiel was the father of Zerubbabel.

Zerubbabel was the father of Abiud.

Abiud was the father of Eliakim.

Eliakim was the father of Azor.

Azor was the father of Zadok.

Zadok was the father of Akim.

Akim was the father of Eliud.

Eliud was the father of Eleazar.

Eleazar was the father of Matthan.
Matthan was the father of Jacob.
Jacob was the father of Joseph, the
husband of Mary.
Mary was the mother of Jesus, who is
called the Messiah.

Matthew 1:1–16

ABOUT THE AUTHOR

Francine Rivers has been writing for more than twenty years. From 1976 to 1985 she had a successful writing career in the general market and won numerous awards. After becoming a born-again Christian in 1986, Francine wrote *Redeeming Love* as her statement of faith.

Since then, Francine has published numerous books in the CBA market and has continued to win both industry acclaim and reader loyalty. Her novel *The Last Sin Eater* won the ECPA Gold Medallion, and three of her books have won the prestigious Romance Writers of America Rita Award.

Francine says she uses her writing to draw closer to the Lord, that through her work she might worship and praise Jesus for all he has done and is doing in her life.